"You're a remarkable woman, Charlotte Bennett."

The compliment made her lean back. "Pardon me?"

"You're committed to these kids, aren't you?"

She told herself not to let him see how his words affected her, but she was pretty certain he must have seen the way her mouth went slack, the way she had to look away for a second because she was so touched that he understood.

"They're my whole life."

Olivia took a toddling step toward the kitchen, and they both watched, Charlotte glad to see the avid curiosity on her face.

"No kids of your own at home?"

"No," she said quickly. And there never would be.

She started to back away, her heart pounding in her chest for some reason. "I'll give you a call tomorrow. See how it went."

She couldn't get out of there fast enough, not when it occurred to her that if she'd had a different past, Maverick would have been exactly the type of man she'd have picked.

Dear Reader,

I'll admit, when I came up with the idea for *Home on the Ranch: The Rancher's Surprise*, I wasn't sure if I could pull it off. A man discovering his name was on a birth certificate when he knew there was no possibility it was true? Did that happen in real life?

Fortunately, I had a friend who works in social services. Shout-out to Rojana! She connected me with a coworker who explained the ins and outs of child welfare. Shout-out to Jennifer! I learned that my fictional situation wasn't just imaginary—it happens all the time.

I knew it would require a special man to take in a child that wasn't his own. Maverick Gillian has always known what he wanted—to manage Gillian Ranch, and perhaps settle down one day with a wife and kids of his own. But caring for someone else's child? Suffice it to say that wasn't part of the plan.

Enter Charlotte Bennett, a woman committed to helping foster children find homes. She's seen and heard it all, so when Maverick denies paternity, she's skeptical at first. But as she spends time with Maverick and little Olivia, she realizes he might just be telling the truth...and that he's like no other man she's met before.

Could Maverick be the one to unlock the secrets of Charlotte's past? Will Charlotte learn that love can heal even the most damaged heart? You'll have to read on to find out.

As always, I sincerely hope you enjoy the story.

Pam

HOME *on the* RANCH

THE RANCHER'S SURPRISE

— ⚒ —

PAMELA BRITTON

HARLEQUIN® HOME ON THE RANCH

Recycling programs
for this product may
not exist in your area.

ISBN-13: 978-1-335-00559-5
ISBN-13: 978-1-335-63394-1 (Direct to Consumer edition)

Home on the Ranch: The Rancher's Surprise

Copyright © 2019 by Pamela Britton

Printed in U.S.A.

With more than one million books in print, **Pamela Britton** likes to call herself the best-known author nobody's ever heard of. Of course, that changed thanks to a certain licensing agreement with that little racing organization known as NASCAR.

But before the glitz and glamour of NASCAR, Pamela wrote books that were frequently voted the best of the best by the *Detroit Free Press*, Barnes & Noble—two years in a row—and *RT Book Reviews*. She's won numerous awards, including a National Readers' Choice Award and a nomination for the Romance Writers of America Golden Heart® Award.

When not writing books, Pamela is a reporter for a local newspaper. She's also a columnist for the *American Quarter Horse Journal*.

Books by Pamela Britton

Home on the Ranch: Rodeo Legend
Home on the Ranch: Her Cowboy Hero

Harlequin Western Romance

Rodeo Legends: Shane

Cowboys in Uniform

Her Rodeo Hero
His Rodeo Sweetheart
The Ranger's Rodeo Rebel
Her Cowboy Lawman
Winning the Rancher's Heart

Visit the Author Profile page
at Harlequin.com for more titles.

This one's for my amazing editor,
Johanna Raisanen, who's been with me through
more books than I can count. Johanna, I appreciate
how you never bat an eye when I call my hero
by someone else's name, and when I use *blonde*
instead of *blond,* and that you taught me the
difference between *equestrian* and *equestrienne.*
I hope you know how much your kind words have
meant to me over the years. Thank you for all
you've done to improve my writing and my stories.

Chapter 1

Some days Charlotte Bennett just wanted to chuck it all and become a professional dog walker. Today was one of those days.

"Is it over yet?" she muttered, rubbing her temples.

"I know, right?" Susan, the receptionist at Via Del Caballo Child Protective Services, peeked her head into Charlotte's office. "And it's about to get better." She paused for effect. "He's here."

Charlotte released a deep sigh. "Already? That was fast."

The brows above Susan's blue eyes lifted. "I know."

At least he'd shown up. "What's he like?"

Hard to sum up a man after meeting him just one time, Charlotte knew, but Susan had a sixth sense when it came to people. Maybe it was her gray hair—she claimed she'd earned every strand. Maybe it was her nurturing nature, perfect for someone who dealt with the heartache and chaos of rescuing children. Susan liked to say the eyes were the windows to a person's soul, and she was pretty good at peeking through the glass.

"He seems...nice." Susan tipped her head, her page-boy hairstyle brushing her shoulder. "Upset, but nice."

Maverick Gillian had every reason to be upset. It wasn't every day that a man discovered he was the father of a little girl.

"Go ahead and bring him in."

Susan nodded, but there was an odd tinge to the woman's half smile, one that reminded Charlotte of someone right before they delivered a punch line. She wondered about it, but only for a moment, because a few seconds later their guest stood in her office doorway and she knew the root of Susan's bemusement.

Maverick Gillian was *hot*.

The thought, so unprofessional, so completely out of character for her, jolted her like the sudden jerk of a roller coaster ride. He stood there, hesitant, looking out of place in his light blue shirt and denim jeans—as if he'd just ridden in from the range and his horse was tied up outside. Just staring at him made a flush spread up her neck and into her cheeks, and she realized he was waiting for her to invite him in or to do something other than stare up at him, frozen, and silently gawk.

She shot up out of her chair. It flew backward, colliding with the window behind it. The heat in her cheeks had likely turned into crimson stains of humiliation at the seriously amateurish display. She grabbed the chair, rolled it toward her, turned and pasted a smile on her face.

"Mr. Gillian. Come in," she said as she sat down.

"Miss Bennett." He took off his straw cowboy hat, sat down and then settled the hat on his lap, but she noticed he fiddled with the edge. She knew how he felt. Thank goodness for the buffer zone the desk provided.

"Thanks for coming down so quickly."

"Of course." His eyes were wide. He fidgeted for a moment. "I've been thinking about it the whole way here and, like I said on the phone, this has to be some kind of mistake."

Dark hair and eyes that weren't just blue—they were shock-you-with-their-intensity blue—stared at her imploringly. A day's growth of beard surrounded a mouth far too sensual to belong to a man. The razor stubble chased his jawline and dipped partly down his neck. His brows were so low and thick and his eyelashes so dark they added even more punch to the color of his eyes.

"I know this must come as a shock." She forced herself to take a deep breath. "But I assure you, it's no mistake."

She absently reached for the file resting on her desk. The name Olivia Gillian was spelled out in Arial font across the tab and she stared at it for a moment, recalling the home they'd pulled the child out of two days ago. That must be why she felt so off balance. Lack of sleep. As the director of Via Del Caballo Child Protective Services, she'd seen some bad situations before, but Olivia's living conditions had been one of the worst. Rotting food. Drug paraphernalia. And a stench of filth that had clung to the toddler when they'd removed her from the home. It had broken Charlotte's heart.

"From what we've been able to glean, Rebecca Templeton, Olivia's mom, was in the process of filing a paternity suit against you, but she never completed the process."

"But…that's impossible. I mean, we never… We didn't." He stared at her for a moment, clearly trying to gain control of his emotions. "I swear I never touched Becca."

It wasn't the first time she'd heard words like that. She answered them with the same question she always asked. "So why do you think she named you as the father of her child on the birth certificate? And why does the child have your last name?"

"I don't know. Desperation, maybe?"

"Did you know Rebecca?"

What a stupid question to ask. Of course he'd known her. She'd verified that this morning. She felt her chest flush in embarrassment.

"I mean, she must have had some reason to think…"

"No, she did not. I assure you. Yes, I was with her at a bar once upon a time, but that was, gosh, at least two years ago, and that was the last time I saw her. She got a little too drunk. I drove her home, but that was it. Nothing happened."

She'd heard *that* before, too. It remained to be seen if it was actually true. "We found your cell number in her phone."

"Well, yeah. I mean, we went to high school together. She was a friend, at one point my best friend, but that was a long time ago." He grew more flustered, looked down at his hat and spun it around in his hands in the manner of a man who sought words he couldn't find.

"Your best friend?"

He looked up, nodded, regret in his eyes. "We were pals up through grade school."

She leaned forward. "Mr. Gillian, did Rebecca Templeton ever try and contact you in the past two years? We looked through her phone but didn't see any recent calls."

She watched him carefully. He might make her feel small and ridiculous and wholly feminine, but he was just a man, and she knew firsthand not to trust them.

This man looked her straight in the eye when he said, "Once. After the bar. It was clear she wanted to hook up." She watched him grow more and more tense with each word. "But I told her no. Never heard from her again."

If only she had a dollar for every man who'd denied paternity who turned out to be lying she'd be a rich woman. But this man seemed to be genuinely distraught. His eyes had lost focus for just a split second as he looked back through time, but it was long enough for her to see sadness in his gaze.

"Well, I'm sorry to tell you this, but you are named as the father."

He leaned back as if the weight of the world had been suddenly thrust upon his shoulders, and she supposed in a way it had. He toyed with the hat again.

"What's her name?"

"Whose name?"

"The child."

"Olivia." She fiddled with the sheet of paper in front of her. "About a year and a half old, so the timing fits."

"Yeah, but like I said, there's no way."

She nodded. "We'll have to perform a paternity test. In the meantime, you're Olivia's dad, according to official documents."

"But I'm not."

She gave him her most professional smile. She'd dealt with this type of situation before, too.

"I've done a preliminary record search. Rebecca's mom and dad are both deceased. No siblings. There's nobody to take care of the child."

"But you can't just name someone as the father of your child when it isn't true."

"Unfortunately, you can, Mr. Gillian, but it's your

word against Rebecca's—or Becca, as you call her—and so until we sort it all out…"

"I'm on the hook?"

She pressed her hands against her desk. "Not exactly. We can keep her in emergency foster care for now. I'll ask for a dependency court judge to order a paternity test. It'll involve going to court, but I'm afraid there's no way to avoid that."

"So I'm gonna be dragged into this whole mess whether it's true or not?"

"Pretty much."

"Son of a—"

She moved the file closer to her and opened it. "But if you're refusing custody, that's okay. I can take care of it from this end."

Why had she said the words that way? Like a challenge. Her job must be getting to her. Too many children and not enough foster parents to go around. They'd had to put Olivia with an older woman only ever used as a last resort. It wasn't that she wasn't an authorized caregiver, just that she wasn't as spry, and it was getting harder for her to care for kids, especially little ones. She'd assured Mrs. Johnson it would be temporary. Clearly she'd been wrong.

"I think…" he said and took a deep breath. "I think I should maybe consult a lawyer."

"You're certainly welcome to do that. I even have the number of a family counseling center. In the meantime, I'll try and find permanent lodging for little Olivia."

"So what happens now?"

She shrugged. "I'll make some calls. But you don't need to worry. We'll handle it."

She hoped. It was anyone's guess these days if they'd

find someone to care for Olivia, and the realization that she had yet another kid in need filled her with frustration.

"What happens if you can't find someone?"

"That won't happen. Worst-case scenario, she'll go to a group home."

"You mean like an orphanage?"

"Not exactly. Those don't exist anymore. But like I said, you don't need to worry about it, Mr. Gillian. The next time I see you will be in court." She didn't mean to alarm him, but the muscles in his neck grew tense. "It's standard procedure. You're denying paternity. That's your right. You'll have to go to family court to prove it. You should receive a subpoena within the next few weeks." She stood. "Thanks for coming in."

But he didn't stand up and she found it hard to breathe all of a sudden, because there it was again, the sadness.

"What happens if I take her and then later, when we verify I'm not her father, what happens then?"

Surprise held her hostage for a moment. She slowly sank back down. He couldn't possibly mean…

"Well, that's up to you. You could give her back to us, or you'd have the option of adopting her, but there's no need to go through all that. If you're not her father there's no sense in involving you any further."

She'd seen so many people like him over the years. Aunts. Uncles. Fathers. Mothers. People tasked with the choice of caring for a child or sending those children into the foster care system. Once upon a time she'd been one of those children. She always tried to remain impersonal, and usually she did a good job, but for some reason she held her breath as she waited for Maverick to respond.

"Becca was a friend," he said, looking down at his hat. "Once upon a time a really good friend. I knew she was in bad shape. I should have done something that night when I ran into her in the bar."

"Mr. Gillian."

"Maverick," he absently corrected.

"Maverick, none of this concerns you if what you say is true."

His head shot up. "How hard would it be to take care of a child?"

She almost laughed. "You're kidding, right?"

His eyes had narrowed in seriousness. "No."

"It's a lot of responsibility."

"Yeah, but what if I have help? I have a lot of family."

"It's still a huge responsibility, Maverick. And if you're serious, I would encourage you to take some time to think about it."

He went completely still, and she felt like she was being scanned by infrared. "How does it all work? I mean, I assume you don't just hand children over."

"Well, I'd have to approve you as a nonrelated extended family member. There are forms you'd need to fill out and questions I'd need to ask, and I'd need to sign off on your place of residence. It's a process."

He held her gaze for a long moment. "What kind of questions?"

Was he really ready to go down this road? What kind of man would do that? If what he said was true, if he really wasn't the father, it made no sense. And if he really *was* the father and he was willing to take the child, why didn't he just admit to paternity?

"Well, where would you live with Olivia?"

"I have a home. It's on our family's ranch. Gillian Ranch."

Her spine snapped upright. Gillian Ranch? Holy...

How had she not made the connection? This man was Via Del Caballo royalty. Part of the Gillian family, locals who'd made themselves famous in the sport of rodeo. For the first time she began to wonder if maybe he was telling the truth. Maybe he really wasn't the father. His family money would be powerful motivation to name him as dad. She'd seen it before. Charlotte struggled to remember what else they did. Horses, she thought. They raised them. And grapes. They had a vineyard. Money. Lots and lots of money.

"Do you have a job?"

"Of course."

"Doing what?"

"I work the family ranch."

Of course he did. "Steady income?"

"Yup."

"Any felonies, convictions…?"

"Nope."

This was silly. "Look, if you're really considering this, why don't I give you the next twenty-four hours to think about it? Then I can grill you."

"Twenty-four hours." His intense blue eyes held her own in a way that made her want to look away.

"Do you need more than that?"

"I don't know." He shook his head, breaking eye contact and looking at the ground. "I honestly don't know what the hell I'm thinking."

But he wanted to help. That much was clear. Good-looking *and* bighearted.

She took a deep breath. "Would it help if you met her?"

"When?"

"Today, if I can arrange it."

He leaned forward, rested his elbows on his knees, hat still dangling from his fingers. "I think I should."

She'd give the man points for going the extra mile, but she doubted he'd actually go through with it. No man in his right mind would take on the task of caring for a child who wasn't his own. Unless there was a chance he was lying. But, no, she'd begun to think he really *wasn't* Olivia's father. Then again, she'd been fooled before.

"Just give me a minute to make some calls." She forced a smile.

"How about you let me know when she's here?" He played with the hat again and she noticed his sleeves were rolled up, a dusting of thick hair atop his hands.

She felt her heart do that odd little flip again. "Sounds good."

He stood up and turned, leaving in his wake a masculine musk that brought to mind brown sugar, oatmeal and hard work. She sank back into her chair, clutched the arms of it.

He's just a man. A good-looking, softhearted, do-the-right-thing kind of man. Nothing unique about that. Except they were rare in her world.

For the first time she wondered if she might have found a man she could actually like.

Chapter 2

What the hell was he thinking?

Maverick stared out the front windshield of his truck, wondering if he should call someone, anyone, and talk about what he'd just sort of agreed to. His dad would lose his mind, that was for sure. He should call his aunt. She would lend a sympathetic ear. But, frankly, he didn't want to speak to anyone, so he stared at his phone on the seat next to him and tried not to feel as if he stared into the eyes of a mountain lion instead of an electronic device.

Only when his knuckles started to hurt did he realize he'd been clutching the steering wheel of his F-350 so hard the seam of the leather bit into his flesh. In the back seat of his truck, Sadie whined, as if sensing her master's distress.

"I'm insane for even entertaining the notion," he told the dog.

Sadie cocked her head sideways, her blue eyes so in-

tense it was like she tried to translate his human words
into her canine language. She shook her head, strands of
white-and-black hair flying into the air, perfectly spot-
lighted by the sun's morning rays.

"This whole thing is crazy."

He'd gotten a call at the crack of dawn. Sheriff's office. He might have thought it was a joke except Bren
Connelly was a personal friend. He'd told Maverick to
call Via Del Caballo Child Protective Services ASAP because they were looking for him. And then he'd broken
the news about Becca. Maverick had clutched his phone
so tight it surprised him it hadn't broken.

That night in the bar, he'd been shocked by Becca's
condition. She'd come on to him. He'd told her no. She'd
been upset. He'd insisted on taking her home, and he'd
been appalled at her living conditions, too. And yet he'd
let her go.

And now she was dead.

The guilt of that night stayed with him all day, and it
was part of what made him head back to Via Del Caballo
Child Protective Services a few hours later. Charlotte had
called to tell him Becca's little girl was available for him
to meet. He'd almost changed his mind a dozen times on
the way over, but in the end, he ignored the cold sweat
that trickled from the brim of his cowboy hat as he stared
at an office that had clearly been a single-story home at
one point in its past. He'd let Becca down. He should at
least meet the little girl.

"Mr. Gillian, you're back." Susan, the receptionist he'd
met earlier, was all smiles, and he realized he'd walked
into the office and hadn't even realized it. "I'll let Charlotte know you're here."

He decided to stand and wait for her, his eye catching on the poster of a giggling baby.

His gut kicked.

"Maverick." Charlotte smiled. "Thanks for coming in."

The woman he'd met earlier walked toward him, her soft-looking hair pulled up and off her face in a bun. She looked like someone who threw her entire self into her job, the ivory shirt she wore a wrinkled button-up. Strands of baby-fine hair had popped free. She wore no makeup, but she had a wide mouth made even more generous by the width of her smile. Brown brows spread across the breadth of her equally brown eyes, and they were her best feature, he decided, those eyes.

"I'm not early, am I?"

She shook her head. "Not at all." A flash of perfectly white teeth peeked out. "She's in here."

She motioned for him to follow, and he found it hard to move all of a sudden. This had to be the worst idea of his life.

It'd only be temporary, he reassured himself.

"Maverick, this is Jane Johnson." She turned to an older woman who looked like a relic of the sixties, long gray hair and some kind of loudly colored dress. "And this is Olivia."

His gaze dropped to the toddler standing by the woman's leg.

Becca.

The similarities were another sucker punch to his gut. The tiny little girl—barely even a toddler, by the looks of it—stared up at him out of Becca's gray eyes. She seemed wary, maybe even afraid, as she swayed on stubby little legs. Her brown hair had recently been washed. He could tell by the flyaway strands that stuck out at all angles.

She all but hid behind Jane's legs. For the first time he wondered what it'd been like for her with Becca as her mom. He'd seen pictures of drug houses, and he knew, there at the end, Becca had been hitting them pretty hard. Lord help him, he couldn't even imagine.

He squatted down. "Hello, Olivia."

The toddler shrank back. She wore jeans that were too big for her and a shirt that was also overly large, one with a cupcake on the front, and even though she was too young to converse, Maverick could see she was clearly afraid of him.

"I don't think she's used to interacting with adults," said Mrs. Johnson.

"When we found her, she was locked in a room," said Charlotte.

He looked up at her sharply, and he didn't bother to hide how upset the words made him. The child had been treated like an animal.

Oh, Becca...

"She ate like a wild thing this morning," said Mrs. Johnson. "Poor dear."

The shirt was too big because she was so skinny. No, starved. She might be young, and she might only be a toddler, but he could see the fear and uncertainty in her eyes.

"How...?" He had to swallow over a sudden lump in his throat. "I mean, why?"

He didn't know what he was asking, knew his words didn't make any sense. He stood up again, never taking his eyes off Olivia.

"It happens far more often than you might think," Charlotte said, clearly understanding him. "The mom gets addicted to drugs. She doesn't care for the baby. To be honest, Olivia's lucky she made it out alive. A lot of them don't." Charlotte came forward, bending down by the little girl. She smiled, and Maverick realized Charlotte's whole face transformed when she stared into the eyes of a child. "But she'll be okay, won't you, kiddo?"

He had to blink a few times to get his thoughts in order.

"She's been really good," Jane said. "Went right to sleep when I put her down for a nap this morning."

"Are you okay?"

It was Charlotte who had spoken. She'd taken a step toward him, too, and he hadn't even noticed.

"I'm fine."

But he wasn't. Something about the way Charlotte had looked at Olivia made him realize what he was in for. This wasn't like Sadie out in his truck. This was a living, breathing human being, one who had already suffered so much.

Because of you.

The thought wouldn't leave him alone even though he knew deep down inside he wasn't to blame. He'd been the worst sort of friend. He should have intervened when they were teens and she'd started to drink too much. And then later, when he'd had a chance to help her again, he'd walked away for a second time. Hell, he'd refused to take her calls. Of course, she'd been hoping to lure him back to her side, but still, he could have done something more.

And she had a daughter.

"I think I should take her," he heard himself say.

He saw Charlotte's pupils flare. "Really?"

He already regretted his words. But he'd said them and it felt right.

"Becca was a friend. I should take care of her kid."

At least for as long as they needed him. He had no

idea how long that might be, but he supposed it didn't matter. He was in it for the long haul, or until they found a permanent home for her.

Charlotte placed a hand on his arm, and her touch soothed him in an odd way, especially with those pretty eyes of hers shining their light on him. "I can't let you do this. Not without thinking it through. We have no idea how long it might take to place Olivia with a permanent foster home. It could be tomorrow. It could be next month or the month after that. It's a huge responsibility. That's a lot to ask."

"I've already thought about it. That's all I've been doing since I left earlier, thinking." Time would tell if it was a good idea or a bad one. "And I really think I owe it to Becca."

Her eyes held his own and her gaze softened, and she stared up at him with such intensity it rooted him to the spot. He saw surprise and uncertainty on her face, and also relief, and he wondered just how desperate she'd been to find Olivia a home.

"I still think you should sleep on it."

"I won't change my mind."

The relief turned into something else. A reluctant sort of approval. He realized she had the world's longest lashes.

"All right, then. Let's get the ball rolling." She turned toward the other woman in the room. "Thanks for bringing her in, Jane."

"My pleasure."

Charlotte turned away. He nodded at Jane, his gaze catching on Olivia next.

He'd never been so afraid in his life.

Chapter 3

The man was either crazy or a saint or stupid, Charlotte thought.

Or he could really be Olivia's father.

But she just didn't think that was true. She didn't know why, but she didn't.

"You know this will be a process, right? Even with emergency placement there's still paperwork to fill out. And I'll have to do a formal interview and a background check, and I'll have to inspect your home. You'll need to shop for supplies, too, most especially a car seat, not to mention food and clothing and a bed for the child."

He looked dazed. Poor guy.

The thought, sympathy for a man, was so foreign to her that she froze for a moment. She didn't usually care what a man felt.

"So what's the next step to become an emergency

caregiver?" he asked. "And I presume my role would be temporary, right?"

"It would be." Charlotte led him back to her office. "Right now she'll go back home with Jane until we get all the details ironed out."

"So she won't go home with me today?"

"Well, she could, but I still think you should sleep on this. We'll get the ball rolling from our end, and if tomorrow you feel the same way, we can do the home inspection then."

She spotted relief in his eyes, not that she blamed him. He'd just agreed to take on a Herculean task. She wouldn't be doing her job if she didn't slow things down a bit, though, let him have some time to think things over along the way. Jane could care for Olivia for a day or two.

And if he didn't change his mind?

She'd count herself lucky. One less child to worry about, at least for now.

"Why don't you have a seat and we'll get started."

He took a few steps and then stopped. Jane had emerged from the room behind him, Olivia in her arms. He stepped toward her and smiled at Olivia. "I'll see you soon," he said gently.

The child was too young to do anything but simply hide her head in Jane's shoulder, and Charlotte felt a familiar sickness roll through her. She went as still as the little girl. She, too, knew what it was like to be afraid. Fortunately, Olivia was young, and in time she would forget what she'd seen and endured, but not Charlotte. She would never be able to forget...

"Ready?"

She shook herself back to the present. Maverick stared at her oddly, and she realized he'd turned toward her and she hadn't even noticed. Jane's gaze caught her own. The woman knew her background, and she'd spent enough time with her to be able to read the emotions Charlotte had let float to the surface. Her look of concern prompted Charlotte to force a smile.

"Follow me," she said. "Jane, you can take Olivia home if you want."

The foster mom nodded, but she still stared at Charlotte in concern. There'd be questions later. Jane had been one of the first foster parents to befriend her when she'd started with CPS. She knew about her time spent in the foster care system, and she knew how deeply it had affected her.

"I'll see you later," she told her, hoping the smile she'd pasted on her face was enough to preempt any questions.

"Have a seat," she said for the second time, once more glad for the barrier of her desk. He wasn't the first good-looking man who'd walked into her office, but he was the first to make her feel like a silly teen.

"How long until we get the paternity test back?" He took his hat off again, resting it on his knee.

"Not long. A couple weeks at most." She brought Olivia's file up onto her desktop. "If you volunteer for one it takes less time. Otherwise, I'll have to order one through the courts."

"Then I volunteer."

She met his gaze. He was not Olivia's father. She knew it with a certainty that took her breath away, given how jaded she'd become over the years.

"Terrific. Let me give you the name of the medical center where they can test your DNA."

She took a piece of paper and noticed her hands shook as she wrote down the information. It disturbed her.

There were so many walls around her emotions it was unusual to have a reaction like this. It bothered her. As the CPS coordinator for his case, she shouldn't be forming opinions about the man. She needed to remain detached and focus on Olivia.

"Thanks," he said when she slid him the piece of paper. "I'll head over after we're done."

"Good. Then let's get started on the basics."

It took her the better part of a half hour to get through the Q&A process, and then another half hour to go over what would be expected of him. Background check. Legal process. Home inspection.

"When do you want me to inspect your home?" she asked.

"Anytime you want."

"Well, the sooner I take a look at your place, the sooner I can designate you as a NREFM."

He stared at her blankly.

"A Non-Related Extended Family Member." Once again, talking shop helped her to regain her focus. "As a friend of the deceased parent, you're a perfect candidate for foster parenting. The court looks more kindly upon family friends taking custody of orphan children."

"Orphan." His fingers found the brim of the hat, fiddling with it. "Are you sure she has no one?"

"I'm certain. It's part of what we do here, look for family members."

He straightened. "Well, Olivia has me."

She peered at him for a long moment, reading the sincerity in his eyes. She had a fleeting thought that he really was quite remarkable, but then she blushed for some strange reason.

"So, do you have time for me to inspect your home today, then?"

"We can do it now."

She'd had a feeling he would say that. "Terrific. Why don't you give me your address? Should we say four p.m.? That will give you time to call the medical clinic for your DNA test and get started on this list—" she handed him the home study requirements for foster homes "—and me time to get the paperwork started."

"Sounds good to me."

He stood up and she tried not to feel intimidated by the sheer size of him.

Rodney had been tall. She gulped. She hated thinking about him.

"I'll see you later."

How in the hell was he going to explain all this to his family?

Maverick sat outside the home he'd just built, Sadie whining to be let out. He opened the truck door. She crossed his lap and jumped out, Maverick watching absently as she ran to the porch, waiting for him.

If only you knew what your human just agreed to do.

There would be an adjustment period for his dog, too. His heart beat so dang hard he could feel it hammering his neck.

He had to be crazy.

There was no other way to explain why he'd ever agree to care for Becca's daughter… Becca's frightened, poorly dressed, starving little girl.

And he could have done something about it. Could have acted to see if Becca was okay…*should* have done it. But he hadn't. He'd been too busy. Made too many excuses. Had told himself it wasn't his problem. He'd been wrong. But he could do something now.

"You ready for this?" he asked Sadie when he came up to her, bending down to scratch the dog's head. He hadn't mentioned owning a dog and wondered for a moment if that would be an issue, but Sadie was as much a part of the family as anyone.

He straightened, pausing for a moment to study his home, trying to visualize it with a little girl playing in the front yard. He'd built the home for that very reason— to house a family. Set in a small clearing surrounded by huge valley oaks, the single-story farmhouse had taken him years to save up and build. No free handouts for the Gillian kids. His dad believed everyone needed to work for the things they had. Which was why Maverick hadn't landscaped yet—he couldn't afford it. So the ground still bore the scars of the heavy equipment they'd used to clear a pad. It was off a gravel road, one that led to the back pastures, far enough away from his dad's place to give him some privacy, but not so far away that he couldn't walk to family dinners on a Sunday night. It was bigger than he'd planned to build, completely surrounded by a porch on all four sides, the steep angle of the roof housing three dormers along the ridge cap. His little slice of heaven, one about to be turned on its head.

The deep breath he took was meant to fortify his resolve. Didn't work.

"Let's go."

Sadie followed him into the house, watching his every move. He busied himself going through the checklist Charlotte had provided, covering outlets and installing childproof locks on cabinets. It was about the only thing he had to worry about, his home being so new and all.

The other items on the checklist didn't really apply. He lost track of time, and so when he heard someone pull up and Sadie start to bark, he straightened in surprise. A glance at his cell phone revealed she was early.

It wasn't Charlotte. It was his brother Flynn.

"What the heck have you got going on here?" he asked, barging into Maverick's place as if he owned it. His brother's blue eyes swept around the house, catching on the bag of supplies that sat on the kitchen table their brother Carson had made for Maverick.

"Oh, you know." He hoped Flynn didn't see the flush that heated his neck. "Just making sure I'm prepared for when my nieces and nephews come over."

Flynn's thick lashes swooped up, then down even lower, the brim of his cowboy hat dipping down to match. Maverick tried not to panic. He didn't want Flynn to know what had happened, at least not yet. He still wasn't 100 percent sure he'd end up with Olivia. Charlotte would decide if he was fit to take care of her, and until then, he didn't want to set off the equivalent of a familial nuclear bomb.

But Flynn seemed satisfied by the explanation. "You ready to go check on those pairs out back?"

Oh, damn. He'd completely forgotten he'd asked Flynn for help with the mama cows and their babies. No wonder. It seemed like a million lifetimes ago that he'd asked his brother to help.

"Oh, yeah. Right." He snapped his fingers as if he'd just remembered something. "Sorry. Something came up. Won't be able to check them today. Can we do it tomorrow?"

His brother shrugged. "Your deal. Tomorrow works."

If he wasn't housing a little girl. And if he was… Then

what? His stomach wheeled around like a bucking bull. He couldn't even fathom…

"You okay?"

"Tummy bug," he improvised. "Decided to lie low today. Wouldn't get too near if I was you."

Flynn took a step back. Maverick hoped the relief he felt wasn't too obvious.

"Call me tomorrow if you're—"

The sound of another car pulling up interrupted his speech. Flynn's eyes narrowed.

"Stomach bug, eh?"

Think, Maverick, think.

"Friend coming over."

Maverick could tell the direction his brother's mind had taken, and that his reasons for staying home this afternoon had nothing to do with him being sick. He had half of that right.

"Anyone I know?"

"Nope." He got up, trying to usher his brother to the door. "This is actually more of a business call."

"Yeah, right."

His brother was probably thinking he'd arranged an afternoon tryst, but that was better than him learning the truth. Maverick forced a smile and all but thrust his brother out the door.

"Well, hello," Flynn said when he spotted Charlotte.

"Hi," Charlotte said, greeting them both. She had a binder in her hand, the button-down shirt she wore, mussed hair and no-nonsense high heels screaming anything but "romance."

"Charlotte, this is my brother Flynn."

"Flynn. Hi," she said, that smile of hers once again

transforming her face. "I presume you're here for moral support."

Flynn glanced at him sharply. "Moral support?"

No. No, no, no.

"Well, sure," Charlotte said, her smile even bigger. "It's not every day someone decides to become a father."

Oh, damn.

Chapter 4

Charlotte knew she'd said something wrong the moment the words came out of her mouth.

"Father?" Flynn said, swinging to face his brother, brows lifted, mouth having gone slack for a moment before he pressed it closed.

"It's not what it seems." Maverick raised his hands, clearly hoping to stave off questions.

His brother's brows lifted again before his blue eyes met hers.

"I'm so sorry," Charlotte said, and her face felt so hot it was like she'd just opened an oven. "I didn't mean—"

"It's okay." Maverick stepped in between them. "I'll explain everything later." He shoved his brother toward his truck.

"Oh, now, wait a minute—"

"Later," Maverick said sternly, clearly pushing harder. "Right now I need to talk some things over with Charlotte."

"But—"

"I'll explain everything tonight."

"Did he knock you up?" the brother said to her.

If she'd thought her cheeks were hot before, it was nothing compared to now. "Goodness, no."

"It's not like that." Maverick had clearly lost patience with his brother.

"I'm with Child Protective Services," she clarified.

"CPS?" asked Flynn.

"Yes," Maverick answered for her. "And it's not what you think, so don't even go there, either."

Flynn lifted his hands in supplication. "Okay, fine. I'll let you go, but I expect the full story later."

"You'll get one. And don't go telling the family about this, either, not until things are ironed out."

The two brothers stared at each other, and Charlotte had a feeling there was a battle of some sorts going on.

"I mean it, Flynn. Not a word."

"I'll come back later," his brother said, heading toward his truck. "Nice meeting you, Charlotte," he called over his shoulder.

She lifted a hand, but the man was already inside a vehicle that probably cost as much as one year of her salary. The engine rattled to life, and Flynn backed out of the driveway, the tires kicking up gravel.

"I'm so sorry," she said to Maverick as they watched Flynn drive off.

"Don't worry about it. They'll have to be told sooner or later."

He headed toward the house. The sound of his brother's truck faded away into the distance, the ranch so big it was at least a quarter mile to the main facility. She'd been blown away by the place—the vineyards, the fancy horse stable, the gorgeous homes up on a small hill. It was like she'd been transported to Napa Valley with the rolling hills covered by grapes and the horse pastures in the distance. She'd been told to turn right when she got to the heart of the ranch, a gorgeous equestrian facility. Charlotte had done as directed and followed the road a good distance. She'd been wondering if she'd made a wrong turn when his place appeared out of nowhere on her right.

"Is this all new?" she asked, walking up some steps and pausing for a moment beneath a covered porch that surrounded the whole house, or so she guessed.

"It is."

Clearly, the Gillian kids had inherited some of the family wealth, at least judging by the stunning home he led her into. He must have just finished construction. The windows still had the manufacturer's stickers on them. And it smelled like paint, probably the light gray exterior, or maybe the scent came from inside. When he swung the door wide the smell grew stronger, but then she was welcomed by another member of the family, a medium-sized black-and-white dog.

"Oh, hi," she said, holding her hand out to keep the dog from jumping up on her. She'd never been a big fan of dogs, probably because she hadn't grown up with them. She hadn't grown up with a lot of things.

"It's okay. She's friendly. Sadie, down."

The dog instantly sat. "Wow. Impressive."

"I hope she won't be a problem?"

"As long as she's up-to-date on all her vaccinations, she won't be." The white-and-black dog inched forward, her nose sniffing Charlotte's loafers. "And, of course, you'd need to watch her around the baby."

"She's more likely to lick a baby to death than hurt her. Sadie, stop. Leave our guest alone."

The dog obediently backed away.

"She's a border collie, and she's used to my nieces and nephews. Never harmed a hair on their heads."

"Good to know. I'll make a note of it." She turned and looked around. "And this is your home."

"Yes, it is."

And what a home it was. Lucky Olivia. She tried not to feel too intimidated by the sheer size of the place. The house looked average sized from the outside, but not when you walked through the front door. With its raised ceilings and open, airy spaces it seemed huge. Sadie's nails clacked against the hardwood floors, the sound echoing off the ceiling above.

"I just moved in."

"I can tell."

Still decorating. He was low on furniture. He had a couch, but it seemed too small for the family room in front of her. Nothing on the walls, either. Just a few pieces of furniture here and there, but it was all nice stuff, and it certainly confirmed what she'd suspected earlier. Becca might've named Maverick as Olivia's father because he was rich. Well, his family was rich.

"So, let's start right here, then, shall we?" She wrestled with herself to slip on her work smile because no matter how many years it had been, there was still a part of her that feared being alone with a man.

"Looks like you've got the plugs all covered up."

He crossed his arms. Somewhere along the line he'd discarded his cowboy hat, his dark hair mussed, his five-o'clock shadow so pronounced she wondered if he'd forgotten to shave this morning.

"I did. And fixed all the cupboards so they lock now."
He glanced around. "The house is brand-new, so there
really isn't a lot to worry about."

"It's lovely. Did you design it?"

"I did. And built it myself. And paid for it all, including the land. Gillians are expected to earn their keep
around here, despite what you might have heard."

She hadn't been thinking that at all.

Well, okay. Maybe she had.

"It's perfect" was all she could think to say.

And it was. The house was spotless, uncluttered, and
everything in it, from the appliances in the kitchen along
the right side of the house to the furnace in the back, was
in good condition—much of it brand-new. It took less
than an hour to confirm it'd pass inspection, and when
she finished, she turned back to him with a smile on
her face. An hour in his company and she felt every bit
as off-kilter as when she had first arrived, and it was ridiculous because he was not Rodney. All that had been
years ago. She didn't need to think about it ever again,
and yet she felt hyperaware of his presence.

"Can I see the outside?"

"Sure."

What a relief. Maybe a little fresh air would help clear
her mind.

He opened the front door, and Sadie ran off to sniff
the base of a nearby oak tree, the two humans pausing
on the porch.

"It's beautiful out here," she found herself saying.

"It is, isn't it?" He looked around. "I've wanted to build
a home here since I was old enough to walk this far from
my dad's place. I love my family, but I didn't want to be
near my dad and uncle's place, even though my aunt Crys-

tal is the closest thing to a mom I have. It's secluded out here, just the way I like it."

"It is that." She took a deep breath, a sweet scent filling the air, although she had no idea where it came from. She did feel better outside. "Do you have a moment to chat? There are some questions I still need to ask."

"More?" he asked with a teasing lift of his brow.

She had to look away from his brilliant blue eyes. She hated the way he made her feel—as if she had no control over her own emotions.

It was just a physical reaction to the trauma of her past. Lord knew she'd gotten good at recognizing the signs. She'd worked hard to claw her way out of the hole her foster brother had left in her heart. She'd learned the hard way it was better for her sanity if she kept people—especially men—at arm's length. They had a habit of wanting only one thing, and that wasn't something she was prepared to give, ever. Not that Maverick acted like he was interested in her, she thought, looking away and hoping like heck he didn't notice the flush on her cheeks or the way she couldn't hold his gaze for long. The man was probably used to women falling at his feet.

"It's actually the last step of your approval process," she said. "I figure we can get it over with now rather than bringing you back to the office."

The sooner she was done with this man, the better. He disturbed her.

"Sure. Let's go around back. There are some chairs back there."

He led her to the rear of the property, motioning toward some wooden chairs with fluffy cushions on them. They were looking out at his backyard, if one wanted to call it that, because there was no fence, just trees and green grass in the distance, the blades so young and green they were yellowed at the top. There was no lawn, either, and the area around the house was just bare land. She opened her binder and pulled out her pen, feeling better once she put on her professional hat.

"So, tell me about your family."

He considered her words for a moment, and she tried not to feel uncomfortable beneath the intensity of his gaze.

"Not much to tell. Dad's an ex-rodeo star. He breeds cutting horses. Mom died a few years back. My uncle and aunt live on the ranch, too, although their kids, my cousins, all live in town. They own the vineyard. My brothers all live here at the ranch with me. My aunt and uncle still can't believe none of their kids wanted a whole lot to do with this place. My brothers and I, though, we all inherited a love of the land, unlike my cousins. Two of my brothers are married, one of them to a famous race car driver, if you can believe that. They have twins, two of the most adorable kids you'll ever meet. And my sister, Jayden, is married, too, and I have a brother that's engaged."

She'd heard about the stock car racer married to his brother. A celebrity driver who'd opened a race shop in town.

"So, there are already kids on the property?"

"Yup. My brother Carson has two. Well, a stepdaughter and a baby boy. They live in town, but my niece Bella is out here all the time. She's ten. My sister is pregnant, too, but she lives in town. All my siblings are settling down these days. Except for Flynn. I don't think he'll ever get married. He loves his horses too much."

She jotted down some notes, acutely aware of the way her pen sounded as it scratched along the paper. His eyes were on her. She could feel that, too, and it made her want to bury her head.

"What will you do with Olivia while you're working?"

He leaned forward, resting his elbows on his knees, and she pretended not to notice how the movement brought his shirt up tight against his wide shoulders. It was such a strange thing to think, to actually notice the muscles on a man's arms, that she lost control of her pen for a moment. The ink skidded across her paper.

"I was thinking I'd ask my aunt Crystal to watch her. Or I could hire someone. Either way, I think I've got that covered."

"And how do you think your family will react to Olivia being a part of your life?"

It wasn't one of her official questions, but it had tumbled off her lips without thought. He didn't answer immediately, instead turning to stare out over the back of his property. She saw grooves in the corners of his eyes.

"To be honest, it's going to freak everyone out. I know it will. I mean, you saw my brother's reaction. He probably thinks I have an illegitimate child or something when nothing could be further from the truth." He shook his head. "My dad's the one who will really lose his mind. He's been itching to retire for the past year, and now that I'll have Olivia, he's going to think I can't manage the ranch all on my own, but I won't be on my own. Flynn can help and so can my other brothers. I'll just have to convince him it can be done."

Because he wanted to make it work. She could see that in his eyes. He might be terrified of becoming an instant father, but now that he'd made the decision to temporarily take Olivia under his wing, he was committed to the task, no matter the sacrifices he would have to make or the problems it might generate. The realization made her stomach do something weird, made her look away again and wonder how it was that a man like him wasn't already married.

"Are there any lakes or ponds on the property or anything like that?"

Back to official questions, although as a change of subject it was abrupt. She didn't care. Her thoughts were so out of character. She felt like she'd just come off a ride at a carnival. Her head spun.

"There is up the road a bit, but it's fenced off. No way for a child to get to it."

"Will it be okay if I confirm that, and if we talk to some of your family members? Not right this minute, but soon. I'm only approving you for emergency placement, but that still means we'll need character references, and to check your financials and assess family members. Will that be okay?"

"Sure. Just understand my brothers are all characters, especially Carson. Not a serious bone in that man's body."

"I'll keep that in mind." She focused on the next series of questions, and she could tell Maverick would pass the prescreening with flying colors. The man had it all. Nice home. Good income. Large family to help take up the slack. All in all, they'd been lucky.

"What about you?"

She'd been so deep in thought she hadn't even heard his question. "Pardon me?"

"What about your family? What do they think of your career choice?"

She grappled to come up with a suitable retort. She was not comfortable with personal questions, especially coming from a man like Maverick.

A man like Maverick? What did that mean?

"Oh, I don't have any family, but we don't need to talk about my personal life."

He leaned toward her and it was all she could do not to lean back. "Why not? You've grilled me. It's only fair that I learn a little more about you."

Was he flirting with her? No. But he seemed genuinely curious. She didn't know how to react, wasn't used to men questioning her. She made sure to dress in a way and act in a way that was guaranteed to help her go unnoticed. Until now.

"Well, I mean, I just don't like to divulge that kind of information. Professionalism and all that."

"You mean you don't have any family at all?"

"No. I do not." She didn't want him to pity her. She'd done well for herself, all things considered. There was nothing about her life to pity.

"I think we're done here." She stood up.

He grabbed her hand. "I didn't mean to upset you."

And she froze because of the feel of his fingers clasping her own, the way her whole body reacted to his touch and how she shot away. It was like the one time she'd jumped from a high dive, something she'd done on a dare from one of her foster siblings and that, in hindsight, she shouldn't have done. It'd been too high, and she'd paid a price when she'd landed the wrong way and her skin had slapped the water and left welts. But before that, right after she'd stepped off the diving platform and been falling through the air, it had been unlike anything she'd felt before…until now.

"I'm sorry," she said. "You startled me."

He stood, and suddenly they were inches apart. "No, I'm the one that's sorry."

Oh, dear. There it was. That look again. He'd clearly

gleaned her one weakness. She had a hang-up about being touched—with good reason.

"Thank you for being so candid in your responses, Maverick. I honestly don't see any reason you wouldn't be approved for emergency foster care placement."

He stared down at her for a long moment, and she hated that it was hard to hold his gaze and that all she noticed was the spectacular color of his eyes and the way his five-o'clock shadow seemed thicker along his jaw.

"So, does that mean I get Olivia?"

Deep breath. No, not too deep. The smell of him did something to her, too.

"Pending your background check, yes."

"When?"

"Tomorrow."

He didn't look surprised or even scared. Just... determined.

"Well, all right, then. I'll go out and buy a crib and some other supplies."

She took a step back. Distance. That was what she needed. And after tomorrow, she'd be done with him.

Thank goodness.

"And I'll email you a list of things you should probably pick up in addition to the checklist I gave you."

He tucked his hands in his pockets. "Then I guess I'll see you tomorrow."

She nodded. "Tomorrow."

One more day. That was all she had to spend in his disturbing presence. Thank the good Lord.

Tomorrow couldn't come soon enough.

Chapter 5

He'd sure ruffled her feathers, Maverick thought as he watched her drive away, Sadie sitting by his side. Hadn't meant to upset her. Hadn't meant to touch her. He'd just been sitting there answering her questions and wondering about the occasional glimpses of…something he'd seen in her eyes.

"She's an odd one, isn't she, Sadie?"

Sadie looked up at him, her blue eyes so bright with curiosity he knew she tried to figure out if any one of the words he'd said had something to do with her favorite things in life—like food, truck rides and the occasional belly scratch. She rested her head again when she realized it didn't.

"Come on," he said, feeling sorry for her. "I'll go pour you another bowl of kibble, and then we need to go shopping, and I should probably stop by my dad's place afterward and break the news."

Still, knowing he had to tell his family and actually doing it were two different things. As he drove away from a big-box store later that evening—the back of his pickup stuffed with supplies for Becca's daughter—it felt like he had the stomach flu. The whole time he'd been shopping he'd wondered if he was crazy. Sometimes the answer came back yes. And if he thought that, he could only imagine what his dad would think.

The drive back to the ranch seemed to pass all too quickly. Usually the rolling hills and green pastures soothed him when troubled, but the closer he got to the heart of Gillian Ranch, the more nervous he became. He felt like hiding in the vineyard, losing himself in the acres and acres of grapes like he'd done when he was a kid. Instead he passed the Spanish-style stables to his right, ignoring the turn to his place and pointing his truck up the big hill and toward the single-story home that belonged to his dad. The Gillian family home. The back of it overlooked the valley below. His dad had built a terrace held in place by stone archways that had become a gathering spot for the whole family on Sundays. No extra cars were parked out front. That, at least, was a blessing.

"Come on," he said after opening his door so that Sadie could jump out. She knew the drill, heading off to the covered porch in the front. "Stay."

The ranch had been part of a Spanish land grant years ago. His dad's place sat in the same spot as the original family homestead, and the brick arches along the front and back, terra-cotta roof and heavy oak door echoed themes from the past.

"What are you doing here?"

His dad peeked his head around a corner to his right. He'd been in the kitchen, judging by the glass of what

Maverick would guess was iced tea in his hand. His dad still wore his work hat—a straw Resistol that Maverick's mom had bought him what seemed like a million years ago—his bushy gray brows lifted in question.

"Something wrong?"

Maverick snatched off his own hat, hanging it on a peg near the door. His hands shook as he used both hands to smooth back his hair, inhaling a deep breath. His boots echoed on the terra-cotta floor as he headed straight for one of the bar stools that sat beneath a raised countertop. How many times had he sat right here and discussed things that troubled him with his mom? Man, he missed that.

"I need to tell you something."

His dad went around to the other side of the counter, waiting. That was the thing with his dad. He was the quiet type. Half the time it was impossible to know what he was thinking. Just when you thought you'd gone and made him mad, he'd crack a joke or reassure you with a pat on the back. Hard to read. That was what his mom used to say.

"What's the matter, son?"

The quiet reassurance in his eyes was a new look for him. The past few years had changed him. He was more laid-back nowadays, and Maverick wondered if it had anything to do with his brothers and sister getting married.

"Well, Dad, I don't know any other way to say this other than to just spit it out." He took another deep breath. "I've decided to become a foster parent."

His dad just about dropped the glass he held. It made contact with the granite countertop as if his grip had slipped. Maverick wondered if he'd cracked the glass.

"Temporarily," Maverick hastened to add. "It's Becca's daughter, Olivia. She died, Becca did, and I—"

"Wait," his dad interrupted. "Becca died? Your child-hood friend? That Becca?"

He nodded, and the finality of her loss hit him hard enough that he couldn't breathe for a moment. He hadn't let himself think about it...about her...about how she'd died. About how he'd actually lost her twice now, the first time when they were both freshmen in high school—she'd gotten involved with the wrong crowd and he'd had to distance himself—and then now. But this "now" was permanent, and it struck him like a linebacker to the gut.

"What happened?" his dad asked.

"Drugs."

"Drugs?" his dad echoed in disbelief.

His dad hadn't known about Becca's problems. Maverick supposed he hadn't wanted him to know, hadn't wanted his dad to lose respect for her because once that happened there was no going back as far as his dad was concerned. He was that kind of man. Do the wrong thing and he'd write you off. So, Maverick had kept quiet. Still loyal to her even after all these years—only look how it'd all ended up.

"She died and she left behind a little girl." He had to ball his fists to help him keep his cool. He needed to hold it together right now. To explain.

"Olivia's the little girl's name and she's an orphan, Dad, and so they called me because for some reason Becca put me down as the father, only I'm not."

He squared his shoulders and looked his dad square in the eyes. "I'll be taking a DNA test to prove it. I never had a thing to do with Becca, not since we started high school, so don't look at me that way."

His dad pressed his hands against the countertop, his

knuckles blanching from the weight of his body, and his dad knew him well enough to know he told the truth.

"Are you sure this is what you want to do? Taking in a child. Son, that's a big responsibility. You know you don't have to take care of her just because of a name on a birth certificate, don't you?"

He wasn't surprised his dad tried to talk him out of it. "I know that, Dad. I want to do this. I volunteered, actually."

His dad eyed him in such a way that it felt like Maverick's skin was being peeled apart layer by layer. It was clear his dad wasn't thrilled with the idea, but he didn't say anything, and Maverick realized his dad was waiting for him to explain himself further.

"Becca was my friend, Dad. A good friend. I let her down. Not once, but twice. I saw her two years ago. She was in terrible shape, and I could have helped then. If I'd been any kind of true friend, I would have helped her a lot, but I didn't. She even tried to call me after. I refused to take her calls.

"I think she put my name on that birth certificate because deep down inside she knew how it would all turn out, knew she was in too deep, and that I could be counted on to make sure her little girl ended up with the right kind of family." He took a deep breath. "And so I've applied to become an emergency foster parent while the courts work through that process. Olivia will be here tomorrow."

His dad never looked away from him, and he could see tension fade away from his face as the realization dawned that Maverick was really going to do this and that there was nothing he could say to dissuade him. He turned away from the counter, going to a cabinet and pulling out a bottle with amber-colored liquor inside. He poured himself a finger width, then tossed it down.

"Want one?" he asked, his voice raspy from the burn of the whiskey.

"No, thanks." The most he ever drank was an occasional beer. That was what he'd been doing the last time he'd seen Becca, downing one at the Silver Spur after a long day moving cattle. She'd come up to him and at first he hadn't even recognized her. She'd gotten so skinny. Her once beautiful hair had hung in limp disarray around her gaunt face. She'd looked like someone who'd come in off the streets.

"Son, I can't say I think this is a good idea. The chaos this will cause in your life isn't something to be taken lightly, but I'm proud of you for stepping up to the plate." His dad lowered his head and looked up at him through his eyebrows. He had a habit of doing that when a conversation turned serious. "But I do have some questions, like who's going to watch her while you're working?"

He scratched his head. "I figure I'll ask Aunt Crystal. She used to watch Paisley all the time for Jayden. I'm sure she won't mind watching Olivia."

"Yeah, but Paisley is Crystal's niece—well, great-niece. This child isn't even family. And what about those days when Olivia is sick or has a doctor's appointment or whatever?"

"It's temporary, Dad. I doubt I'll have her all that long, but if something comes up, Flynn can step in and help with the ranching operations. Or Carson, if he's around. He might be focusing more on his construction and furniture business, but he can still help."

Another long stare. "Times like these I wonder what your mom would think."

"Me, too."

"This sounds like something she would do. She was always taking in stray animals and volunteering her time. She'd be proud of you, too."

He missed her like hell. They'd been close, the two of them. Truth be told, part of why he'd been so committed to Gillian Ranch was because he knew that was what she would have wanted. She would have loved to help out with Olivia. Heck, she probably would have offered to take the little girl in.

"I just hope you know I'm not the little girl's father."

"I know that," his dad said. "One thing you're not is a liar. Except when you were younger and you left that gate open. Your aunt wrung the truth out of you. Do you remember that?"

"I do," he said with a half smile. "First and last time I ever lied."

"Well then, I guess I'm out of questions. I just wanted to make sure you knew what you were getting into."

"I do. But I'm not going to lie—I'm scared to death. But I know it's the right thing to do. Helping a kid out in need. I'm in a perfect position to do that. I'm self-employed. I have plenty of family to lend a hand. I have a big house. I can take care of her for as long as they need me to."

"And what if it's longer than just a few weeks?"

"Then I'll find someone to help me take care of her. You'll see. I'll be fine."

He hoped.

"Are you sure you're ready for this?" Charlotte asked Maverick the next day, catching the scent of him and immediately blushing for some strange reason. "It's a pretty big deal."

He didn't look any more reassured today than he had yesterday. She could see the worry in his eyes, but his gaze sharpened for a moment.

"Does that mean I've been approved?"

She tried to ignore the musky smell of him. He'd rested his cowboy hat on his right knee, and his hair seemed to be more mussed than yesterday.

"Yup. You've been approved. Background check came back this morning. You're all good."

He leaned back in his chair, and she wasn't sure if it was in relief or so he could muster up some strength to face the coming day. "So, she'll be living with me as of today?"

"That's the plan."

His head lowered, staring at the ground, and she could tell the suddenness of it all surprised him. She slipped out of her chair without really even thinking about it, resting a hip on her desk and crossing her arms.

"You're going to be fine." If she'd been like a normal person, she might have patted him on the shoulder in re-assurance, but talking to him was the best she could do. "You might be surprised how well new parents adapt to taking care of a child. And you said yourself you'll have help. You'll see. It'll be okay."

"When?" She saw him take a deep breath before sit-ting back in the chair again. The pupils in his light blue eyes contracted. "I mean, do I pick her up from here? Or go get her?"

"I'll bring her to you." He seemed relieved. "I need to go over car seats and dietary requirements and things like that. You'll see us both later on today. Should we say four again? That gives you some time to prepare."

"Sounds great." He stood up and they were suddenly

inches away, his hat held in front of him, though he played with it as he faced her. "Thank you."

He held out his hand. She stared at it for a moment before grasping it, and it was like diving off that board again. What sounded like wind rushed through her ears. She froze and for a moment battled complete panic. Then he released her, stepped away and walked out of her office, and she knew he hadn't felt a damn thing. He was just a man, one who'd been compelled to take in a friend's little girl. He wasn't Rodney. He didn't hurt people. And he sure as hell didn't want to do what Rodney had done to her. That was a good thing.

She turned as he left the building, watching him from her office window. She might be damaged by her past, but she could still recognize a good man. This man was kind. And bighearted. A regular stand-up person.

Unlike Rodney. Or her foster father who'd turned a blind eye to everything.

Enough, she told herself. She refused to spend another millisecond thinking about either of them.

She turned back to her desk. But the memory of Maverick Gillian was seared into her mind, like an image stained the back of someone's lids after they closed their eyes. What would it be like to date a man? she wondered. To be kissed by one. Heck, to have one touch her tenderly.

Ridiculous, she thought, tapping the space bar of her keyboard a little too hard. Thank goodness she'd be done with him by the end of the day. Then she'd never have to see him again.

The man was entirely too disturbing for her peace of mind.

Chapter 6

The place was beautiful.

Charlotte had known that, of course, but it struck her again as she drove through the entrance, a rock wall made of earth-toned stones on either side of the road. It seemed to go on and on for miles, rolling green hills on either side of the road, cattle grazing here and there. And then the hills parted and a vineyard covered the valley in front of her, spreading north and south, a Spanish-style barn with a red tile roof to her right, homes up on the hills behind it. The unbelievable majesty of the place took her breath away.

"You're a lucky little girl," she told the toddler in the back seat. Olivia shook the toy she'd been given before their ride, the plastic keys clacking together. She'd been fascinated by it ever since Charlotte had handed it to her, and Charlotte had a feeling she knew why. There hadn't been a single toy in Rebecca's apartment, not even a teething ring. Just empty bottles and cans of formula and a pile of soiled diapers. And the sad thing was, it wasn't even the first time Charlotte had seen something like that.

"Almost there." She pointed her compact car past the swanky stables. She had no idea why she was narrating her journey. Well, maybe she did.

Nerves.

It felt good to talk to someone, even if that someone was a toddler. Glancing into the rearview mirror and seeing that sweet face made her remember she had a job to do, an important job, a job that had gotten her through some of the darkest moments of her life.

He was on the front porch when she arrived, and she wondered if Maverick could tell she'd been approaching from the dust trail her car left behind. She couldn't deny her heart began to pound. Hard to ignore how hard her pulse tapped the side of her neck. But she was always a little nervous when she handed off a child to temporary foster care. One never knew how it would go. She'd even had one young couple change their minds the moment she'd pulled up.

"Sadie, stay," she heard him tell his dog when she opened the door. The black-and-white border collie lay down obediently on the porch, but she stared at the car intently.

"You made it," he said. He smiled, but it was forced, and despite her own discomfort, she felt a pang of sympathy for him. He had to be nervous. She had yet to meet a new foster parent who wasn't.

"Come on over." She waved him over, slipping outside so she could get Olivia out of the car. "I'll show you how to work a car seat."

Just focus on your job, she told herself.

Olivia's head turned toward her, but there was no smile, no look of curiosity. She wore the look of a child who didn't know how to interact with human beings. She should be talking now or at least uttering a few words, but Jane said she hadn't spoken a word. At least she looked better. Her hair was clean, although it hung limply, dull and lifeless—the product of poor nutrition. She wore a pink shirt and a pair of jeans that were too big on her.

"Hey there, baby girl." She smiled down at the toddler whose big gray eyes peered up at her warily. What had the poor little girl endured? It was a question that haunted her. But then Olivia's gaze slipped past her, landing on Maverick. The look of wariness changed to one of curiosity, which made Charlotte think men had been an oddity in Olivia's young life. That, at least, was a blessing because there were some men in the world—

She cut off the thought.

"This is Maverick," she told the little girl. "You remember meeting Maverick, don't you?"

The gray eyes flicked back to her own. Charlotte smiled, motioning for Maverick to move in closer.

"So, most car seats have a central button for parents to push. And from there it's easy to slip the shoulder belts over her. Like this." She demonstrated. "You bought the car seat that was recommended on our list, right?"

"I did."

"Good. Then yours will be just like this. Super easy to use. When you take her someplace, just make sure the seat is secured to your truck's seat belt system like this."

She pointed. "Then slip the belts over her shoulders and hook them together in this plastic thing here."

He'd crouched down next to her and it was like an invisible force field touched her. She had to resist the urge to shy away.

"And when you want to take her out, you unclip the plastic thing first. Then you slip the straps over her shoulders." She gently tugged the child's thin arms through the nylon straps. Poor thing really was half-starved. "Then reach behind her and pull her up and out, but be careful of her head. If you're not careful you can hit it on a doorjamb. Here. You do it."

He stared between her and Olivia like she'd just asked him to recite the alphabet backward. "Right now?"

She found herself on the verge of smiling, which struck her as odd given how nervous he made her feel. "You're going to have to do it sooner or later."

He nodded and inched closer, his big hands reaching for Olivia, a slight smile on his face. "Okay, kiddo, guess this is it. You and me from here on out."

She liked him.

And it wasn't the same kind of like that she'd felt for other men in her past—the foster dads and coworkers and study buddies back in college. It was some kind of extreme form of admiration for a man who had been thrust into a difficult situation and made the best of it. He might be scared to death—and nothing demonstrated that better than the way he tenderly lifted Olivia out of her car seat, like she was precious glass—but still managed to smile at the little girl, perching her on his hip in a way that bespoke a familiarity with kids.

"There," he said. His five-o'clock shadow had turned into full-on stubble, and she wondered if he'd forgotten to shave with everything that'd been going on in his life. "Ready to see the place you're going to call home for a little while?"

Olivia stared up at him, and the expression on her face could only be called *studious* as she examined the new human in her life. She leaned back a bit, ostensibly to get a better view, and when she spotted the short hairs on Maverick's face, she lifted a hand and touched him tentatively, her eyes widening when her fingers made contact with the stubble.

Adorable.

If she'd been the kind of woman to go all soft when a man was kind to children, she would have melted on the spot right then. But she wasn't that kind of woman. She was the kind who would never let herself feel anything about them.

Maverick smiled. "Does that tickle your fingers?"

The little girl drew her hand away, and Maverick turned and beamed at Charlotte next.

"She's so cute."

She's an orphan. A little girl who's just like me. Except she realized in that moment that Olivia had landed in a home as different from the one she'd grown up in as earth was to the heavens, at least temporarily. It made her wish with all her heart that she could convince Maverick to keep the little girl in his care. If she could do that, Olivia would never want for anything in her life. She would never know fear. She would never blame herself for things that happened in her past, things that it might take years for her to understand weren't her fault. Never be afraid of men. Never long for things she couldn't have.

If only...

But what if she could convince him? Wouldn't that

be a small miracle. And that was exactly why she'd gotten into this frustrating, sometimes terrible, sometimes incredibly rewarding business. To do right by the kids who came into her care.

She squared her shoulders, deciding right there and then that she would do everything in her power to convince Maverick to take Olivia on as a permanent foster child. And if that meant spending more time in his company then so be it. She would just have to get over the crazy way he made her feel.

She had the strangest expression on her face, Maverick thought, wondering about it before turning back to the little girl in his arms. Olivia was lighter than he'd expected. Of course, he was used to his brother's kids. Twins. Both of them taking after the Gillian side of the family, which meant big for their age.

"Come on, Olivia. Let's get you inside."

He glanced back at Charlotte, but she'd turned away, reaching for something in her car, emerging with her purse and a folder, a professional smile. He didn't know why, but he had a feeling she'd had to wrestle with herself over something.

"Go on in. I'll follow," she said.

Olivia never took her eyes off him, and he'd be lying if he didn't feel a twinge of fear as he carried her inside. This was it. There was no turning back. Not now. Sure, he could always claim it was all too much, that he wasn't suited for foster parenting. But he wouldn't. When he made a commitment to do something he always saw it through.

"Sadie, stay outside," he told the dog, smiling when he spotted the dog's forlorn expression. "You'll get to meet our guest later on," he promised, leaving the door open so Charlotte could follow. He redirected his smile to Olivia. "These are your new digs."

At least until Charlotte could sort out permanent placement. Surely that wouldn't take long. He'd always heard about young couples who couldn't have kids. Olivia would be a godsend to someone.

"Did you get that baby swing?" Charlotte asked, trying to close the front door, but Sadie tried to slip inside. "No," she told the dog.

"Sadie. Outside."

The dog shot him a look that seemed to say, *You don't really mean that, right?*

"Out," he repeated.

"Wow," Charlotte said. "She really listens."

"She's a good dog. Loves kids. Not sure what she'll think about having one living here all the time, but she'll get used to it. And, yes, I got that swing. I think I got everything on your list."

He wasn't kidding. If it wasn't already unpacked, it was sitting in a box in Olivia's room.

Olivia's room.

His stomach kicked again. The thought of putting the little girl to bed, when there'd be nobody around to guide him, filled him with fear. Maybe he could ask Aunt Crystal to stay the night. Or perhaps one of his siblings wouldn't mind helping.

"Should I put her in it now?"

Charlotte nodded, following him into the kitchen to their right, where he'd set up the swing because that was where he'd seen a similar device in his brother's home.

"Like this, yes?" he asked her, slipping Olivia into the cloth seat. He'd watched his brother do the same thing, but he'd never truly appreciated just how hard it was to fish a little girl's wiggling legs through the tiny holes, especially when she started to kick.

"Whoa there, honey," he told her. "You're like a steer avoiding a heel rope."

"Let me help."

He heard her place her purse and folder on the table, and then she was by his side, her scent filling the air as she leaned down next to him, grinning at the little girl.

"It works best if you just sort of sit her down. Their legs seem to naturally find the holes."

She took Olivia from him, demonstrating, her head lowering until she was nearly nose to nose with the baby. "Like this," she said in a singsong voice. "Now let me strap you in."

It was like looking at a painting in a mirror, seeing things in reverse, the unique perspective of being so close to Charlotte allowing him to see the fine details of her face. The way the creases at the corners of her eyes softened as she stared down at Olivia. How her lips were a soft shade of red that he was pretty sure was natural because she didn't strike him as the type to use makeup. And how she went from no-nonsense and businesslike to slow and gentle, her hand lifting away from the safety belt to gently brush Olivia's hair. The child looked up at her, and the sides of her mouth tipped up.

"Do you see that?" Charlotte gushed. "She smiled."

"She did."

They were both smiling, and for some reason it made Maverick gulp and then draw back. Some crazy thoughts were swirling through his head, and he didn't want to examine them too closely because they made him feel like the lowest sort of life form. Why the heck was he having thoughts about a CPS worker? She was totally not his type. He usually favored the rancher's-daughter type, not a city girl who didn't know the first thing about life in the country.

And yet...

"I can't believe she smiled," she said, straightening. "That's the first grin I've seen from you, huh, Little Miss Olivia?"

He went to his fridge, pulled out a plastic jug of iced tea, set it on the kitchen's center island and poured himself a big glass. She loved kids. So what? Lots of women loved kids. He hoped to settle down with a woman like that, but not for a long while, and not with someone like Charlotte, a woman who was obviously married to her job. It'd just surprised him how different she looked when completely relaxed and happy. That was all.

"I'll take a glass of that, if you don't mind." She leaned against the counter in such a way that she could keep her gaze on Olivia. The little girl had discovered the plastic balls that lined the front of the swing, her eyes widening when she touched one of them and spun it accidentally.

"Has she talked at all?"

And just like that, the light went out of her eyes. "Not a word." She shook her head. "Jane said she tried playing with her this morning, and she acted like she didn't know what to do."

He leaned against the counter, too, noting the differences between Olivia and his brother's kids. Granted, they were a bit older, but he still remembered what they'd been like. Noisy. Into everything. Constantly moving. Olivia acted more like a frightened puppy, one afraid of being scolded, and the sad truth was that she probably was terrified.

"Breaks your heart, doesn't it?"

He turned to find Charlotte looking at him, and he saw a sadness in her brown eyes, one undoubtedly echoed in his own. Yes, she loved kids, but she hated this part of her job, he realized. The part that broke your heart and tore it apart, because Olivia was so little and no child deserved a life like she'd had. That it was Becca who'd done this to her made Maverick sick.

He found himself thinking out loud. "I bet you've seen it all over the years."

She nodded once. "I have."

"You're the director of Via Del Caballo CPS, aren't you?"

She tipped her chin up. "I am."

"I can't imagine having to deal with situations like Olivia's day after day."

Her gaze skittered away, like a creature that tried to hide. "It's a tough deal sometimes."

But he'd seen something in her eyes before she'd turned away, a something that made him think her answer was more personal than she was letting on. He found himself wondering just how deeply her job must affect her. He couldn't even imagine.

"Well, I'll make sure Olivia never wants for anything, at least while she's with me."

Her gaze shot back to his. "I believe you."

Her words were said softly, her eyes so large and dark that they reminded him of melted chocolate. And from nowhere came the thought that he wished his mom was alive to meet her and Olivia. She would have approved of Charlotte and her selflessness.

He straightened, for some reason finding it hard to

speak over a lump in his throat. "You want to take me through meals and such?"

She took a sip of her drink before nodding. "Sure," she said and then set the glass down. "Jane says she seems to like pasta. I don't suppose that was on the menu tonight?"

"I can make her anything you think she might like."

"You cook?"

"I do."

She smiled. "Well, that will make this a lot easier. Just avoid big chunks of food. The main thing with these guys is make sure everything is small enough to be swallowed whole because sometimes it is."

"Are you going to stay and eat with us, too?"

She hadn't really thought about it. Usually she observed a new foster parent for an hour or so, but she hadn't planned on having dinner there.

"I can eat later."

"Why when it's a simple matter of me adding an extra handful of pasta and making a little more sauce?"

She would sound like an idiot if she refused. "Well, if it's really no trouble."

"It's not."

He busied himself fixing a meal, and Charlotte moved back to Olivia, playing a game of peekaboo with her that made the little girl smile once again, and as he prepared the meal he gradually began to relax.

"Smells delicious."

"Fettuccine Alfredo. Super easy. Super fast." He glanced down at Olivia, who watched Charlotte stand up, her eyes following her every move. "She should like it, too."

"At this point, I think she's probably happy just to have three square meals a day."

So sad. He'd known it was bad with Becca, but what she'd let happen to Olivia was unconscionable.

Charlotte frowned. "She could use those extra meals."

Maverick took down plates for them all. He chose a tiny plastic plate for Olivia that he'd had ever since Shane's kids had come over.

"Should I take her out of the swing?"

"You don't have to. You could feed her in it."

"Yeah, but I'd like to try out the new high chair. It's different than the one my sister, Jayden, and my brother Shane have used."

"Then do that. I'm going to wash my hands before I eat."

She let him figure out the swing thing all on his own, Olivia's eyes widening when she caught sight of him hovering over her.

"It's okay, kiddo. I'm not going to hurt you," he whispered.

This whole thing is probably scarier for me than you.

She slipped out of the chair easily enough, and he was familiar enough with high chairs that it was simple for him to navigate. By the time he had her all settled, Charlotte had already scooped up a plate of food, handing it to him.

"Why don't we let her try and eat on her own?"

"Sounds good to me."

He quickly realized he needn't have worried. Olivia clearly knew how to feed herself. She didn't even wait for the plastic spork he'd bought her, just dived into her plate with both hands...literally.

"I think she's got it covered," Charlotte said, smiling. She took a bite of her own food. "Mmm. Yum." She closed her eyes in obvious appreciation of his cooking. "I think I need to bring you home with me."

Her eyes widened, and he could tell she'd realized the words sounded suggestive, her eyes dropping to her plate a second later. "I mean, I've always wanted a personal cook. Someone to cook for me."

"Wouldn't that be nice," he said, trying to set her at ease. "I have a feeling I'm going to be wishing for a nanny by the time this is all over." He smiled at her, taking a bite of his own food. "I'm a little nervous about trying to get out the door in the morning."

She'd blushed a bright red, but the color suited her, her rose-red lips turning a darker hue. She soothed a stray wisp of hair over one ear, and he found himself wondering if she ever wore it down and what it would look like.

"You'll figure it out." She took another bite, but she still refused to meet his gaze. "I know I keep saying that, but you will." He saw her take a deep breath, lift her eyes. "I have faith in you."

"Thank goodness I have a big family that can help."

She nodded. "To be honest, that was a prime consideration when approving your application."

"Do you do that a lot? Place kids into emergency foster care?"

"More often than I'd like, but it's easier with someone like you. You're Olivia's father...according to the paperwork," she quickly added. "There would have been more forms to fill out if you'd declined to care for her."

"You do realize I'm telling the truth about not being Olivia's father."

She stared at him for a long moment, and he knew she was contemplating his words.

"Never mind," he said. "You'll find out the truth soon enough."

"Maverick, I don't mean to insult you. There's a part of me that really does believe you. But what I think doesn't matter. It's up to the courts to decide."

"Is that why I was allowed to take her? Because according to the paperwork, I'm her father? Not because I was willing to help out for the sake of a friend?"

"No. Yes." She shook her head. "The truth is we were so short on foster parents that it was a relief when you volunteered. We're still short on foster parents."

"What if I'd been a total scumbag?"

"Then we would have found that out through the NREFM application process, but you're not a total scumbag, are you?"

"You know I'm not."

He saw something in her eyes then, something that flared within them, but she covered it up by looking away. It made him think she didn't trust him, and if so, why not, and why had she allowed him to take Olivia?

But then she said, "All I know is that long before I'd met you, I'd heard of the amazing Gillian family. But now that I've come to know you, Maverick, I realize just how lucky Olivia is to have you named as her father."

Her words caused him to flush, and he had to look away from her for a moment. He had a feeling she didn't hand out compliments all that often. "I promise I'll be the best temporary dad a man can be."

Again, the long stare before she said, "I'm counting on that, Maverick."

Chapter 7

"She's a mess," Maverick said a little while later, grabbing a paper towel and dampening it beneath the faucet. Charlotte watched and thought he really was good with kids. "Let's get you cleaned up, kiddo."

She had nothing to worry about, she realized. He was a natural at this. Olivia was in good hands, no matter what she might think.

"You want out of there?" he asked when he'd cleaned her up. "You want to explore the house together?"

Charlotte got up, rinsing her plate beneath water, gathering her thoughts before turning to face him. "I think I should probably get going."

He was right in the middle of lifting Olivia out of her high chair, turning toward her with the girl in his arms. "You sure you don't want to stay?"

"I'm afraid I have to leave. I'm behind at work. Need to go home and try and lighten the load."

She turned, looking for her purse. He came toward her, helping Olivia walk alongside of him, but holding on to her hand to steady her. Olivia swayed on her feet, staring up at them both. Then she said, clear as day, "Mama?"

They both froze. Their gazes shot to Olivia, waiting to see what else she'd say, and when Olivia just kept looking around, Charlotte squatted down next to her.

"Are you looking for your mama?" she asked.

She felt Maverick's gaze on her, and her cheeks flushed all over again. It made her angry, not at him but at herself. Here was a classic example of what she was put on this earth to do—help children in need. Olivia clearly missed her mom because she could see the confusion in her eyes as she stared up at yet another new human being in her life.

"Your mama is still here," she told the little girl. She pressed a hand against her chest. "Here. In your heart."

She was too young to understand, and in a way, that was a blessing. Studies showed that children Olivia's age didn't understand death. They understood things like *goodbye* and *hello* and *I love you*, but not something as permanent as a person passing away. Some kids like Olivia cried nonstop for their mothers. Some kids seemed more curious about where their parents had gone, and in Charlotte's professional opinion, Olivia would fall into the latter category. She knew her mother wasn't around, but it didn't upset her. How could you miss something you'd never really had?

"Come give me a hug." She leaned down, placing her arms around the tiny shoulders, feeling her tense at first, then begin to relax, and it made Charlotte want to cry. Heck. Who was she kidding? She could feel her eyes burn with unshed tears. It wasn't fair. Kids like Olivia didn't deserve such a rough start. But Charlotte would see to it that it was only better from here.

"I wish I could take you home with me," she muttered.

"I bet you feel like that with all the kids you help," Maverick said.

She drew back, surprised by the observation. "I do. But it's not feasible." She frowned. "Or realistic."

He nodded, still staring at her. Olivia peered up at them both, no more mention of her mama.

"You're an incredible woman, Charlotte Bennett."

The compliment made her lean back. "Pardon me?"

"You're committed to these kids, aren't you?"

She told herself not to let him see how his words affected her, but she was pretty certain he must have seen the way her mouth went slack, the way she had to look away for a second because she was so touched that he understood.

"They're my whole life."

Olivia took a toddling step toward the kitchen, and they both watched, Charlotte glad to see the avid curiosity on her face. Anything was better than the nearly blank stare she'd seen that first day they'd found her.

"No kids of your own at home?"

"No," she said quickly. And there never would be. She'd survived childhood so she could help out kids who'd been like herself, and nothing, not even kindhearted men like Maverick, would ever convince her otherwise. Marriage? Kids? Not her.

"I think she wants in her swing." She gestured to Olivia, who was pointing at the device. Charlotte started to back away, her whole body quaking for some reason. "I'll give you a call tomorrow. See how it went."

"You want in there, honey?" he asked. But then he turned back. "Thanks for hanging out."

She took another step back. "You're welcome. Good luck." She called to the little girl, waving goodbye, and then turning away without meeting Maverick's gaze. She couldn't get out of there fast enough, not when it occurred to her that if she'd had a different past, Maverick would have been exactly the type of man she would have picked.

"I think it's time you and Sadie got to know each other," he said, the moment Charlotte pulled away from his house. He shifted Olivia to the other hip, his heart pounding in his chest as he held her.

What had he done?

The words were like the lyrics to a song that he couldn't get out of his head.

What had he done and what had he gotten himself into?

"Can you say *dog*?" he asked her.

Not only did she clearly not know the word, but she'd apparently lost her ability to speak, too. She barely moved in his arms, looking around as he headed to the back door, where his dog had been whining.

"This is Sadie," he told Olivia, pointing to the dog behind the glass. Olivia just stared, so he slowly slid the back door open, his dog slipping through the opening no wider than her nose, or so it seemed.

"Hey," he called out. "Sadie, wait."

The collie headed off to the kitchen and the pantry where her food was kept, but she obediently stopped when she heard her name, glancing back at him as if silently asking, *What?*

"I want you to meet Olivia."

Was it crazy to be talking to his dog? Oddly, it made him feel a little less alone in this crazy undertaking of his. Sadie had spotted the little girl in his arms, and damned if she didn't tip her head sideways in obvious puzzlement.

"Sadie, this is Olivia." He squatted down. "Olivia, this is Sadie. Come here, Sadie."

His dog padded over to him quietly, her nose lifted as she tried to catch the scent of the tiny human in his arms.

"Can you say *Sadie*, Olivia?"

The little girl stared at the dog. The dog stared at the little girl, the two of them no doubt sizing each other up and trying to decide if they were friend or foe.

"Or maybe keep trying *dog*. That's a little easier to say for now. *Dog*." He reached for Olivia's hand, gently clasping it and then holding it out to Sadie's nose. "Dog."

Sadie, bless her heart, clearly sensed the child's recalcitrance. When his brother's twins came for a visit, she was all dog smiles and wagging tail. Today she very slowly lifted her nose to the child's hand, touching it and then, after a moment, licking it.

Olivia pulled back and squealed. The movement so surprised Sadie that she wiggled back.

"Was that wet?" he asked Olivia with a smile. "That was Sadie's tongue, but she's not going to hurt you." He grabbed her hand again and held it out to the dog, who did the same thing all over again, which made Olivia cry out and wiggle back. But it wasn't a sound of fear; it was more like…a giggle?

"Is that funny?" he asked her, smiling again, the little girl peering up at him, and something sort of went *ooh* when their gazes connected. It was the strangest feeling, like he stared into his future and his past all at the same time, a sort of déjà vu that took him by surprise.

She looked just like Becca.

He gulped, remembering the pictures of her in her mom's home when she'd been young. It was the smile in her eyes, he realized. Olivia smiled just like her mother had back before the drugs had stolen the life from her.

Becca, Becca, Becca, you damn fool. Look what you're missing out on.

He felt his throat thicken until he took a deep breath that he hoped would push the sadness out of his heart. He had Olivia now. He'd keep her safe, for Becca's sake, and when it was time to hand her over to her permanent foster parents, he'd make sure she stayed safe.

Olivia wiggled in his arms and he realized she wanted Sadie to touch her again. It became a game. He would hold her hand out and Sadie would lick and Olivia would make the strange little noise that wasn't quite a giggle but wasn't a cry of fear, either. And he realized with a flash of heartache that she didn't know how to laugh. That she might not have ever laughed in her life. Was that possible? Could she be so deprived of human company and love that she'd missed out on basic emotions? He had a feeling she had.

Not anymore, he told her silently. Not ever again.

Olivia tired quickly. Or maybe it was just her bedtime. He laid her down on the pink crib he'd bought, the one with the Disney princess blankets, and hoped she wouldn't cry, but all she did was roll over onto her side. He covered her with blankets and she hunkered beneath the quilt, her elbow moving in such a way that he knew she sucked on a thumb.

"You're too old for that," he told her. Or maybe not. Golly. He had no idea. He'd need to consult the parenting book Charlotte had given him or call his sister or someone.

"Good night, sweetie."

She didn't move, just faced the wall, and he held himself still. He had no idea how long he stayed there, but when he leaned forward, peering over her shoulders, he saw the long length of her lashes resting against her cheeks and he realized she was out.

Just like that.

"Well, I'll be damned."

Sadie had followed him into the room, and she glanced at the crib as if surprised to find a new piece of furniture in there. She lifted her head and sniffed the air, and he knew that she knew the tiny little human she'd met earlier was asleep in there.

"Come," he told the dog quietly, padding softly out of the room.

He debated with himself about whether or not to close the door, softly latched it shut, then changed his mind and opened it, then changed his mind again, pulling it almost all the way closed.

"Don't you dare go in there," he told his dog.

Sadie just wagged her tail. And that was that, he thought. Easy.

Except nobody had told him about the worry that came along with being a caregiver. He felt compelled to check on Olivia ten thousand times that night, or so it seemed. She hadn't stirred, but he needed to be sure she was okay, so he kept peeking in on her, wondering if she might try to climb out of the crib. Or if he should have closed the door all the way. What if he couldn't hear her cry out? Or what if Sadie went in there and woke her up? What if, God forbid, she stopped breathing?

He ended up camped out on her floor, Sadie curled up next to him, and he felt like a damn fool because he knew Olivia would be safe. Charlotte would laugh at him if she could see him now. Or maybe not. Maybe she'd approve. He suspected there wasn't anything she wouldn't do for her kids.

That was his last thought before he, too, drifted off to sleep. He never saw his dog get up, pad over to the crib, peering up at the child inside before she, too, curled up beneath the crib, where she would remain sleeping all night.

Chapter 8

She needed to call.

Charlotte glanced at her phone for what must have been the tenth time. As his caseworker, it was her duty to check in on him. It had been a week since she'd had dinner at Maverick's place and not a peep out of him, except for when she'd called the next day to see how his first night with Olivia had gone. He'd reported back that everything had gone great and she hadn't heard a word since. For some reason that surprised her. Then again, he had a huge family to lean on. Still, he hadn't called, which meant it was up to her to make contact.

She glanced at the phone again.

"Oh, to heck with it." She pulled up his records, dialed his number a moment later, a part of her hoping he wouldn't answer so she could leave a message.

"Hello?"

She couldn't breathe for a moment. "Hello," she

echoed, the word coming out in a gush. "It's me, Charlotte."

Could she sound more like a fool? Thank God, he wasn't in front of her watching her cheeks fill with color, something that had become all too common around him.

"Hey," he said in his deep baritone. "How are you?"

"Great...great."

Dumb. She sounded stupid.

"How's Olivia?" she tacked on.

"Terrific," he answered, and then she heard him cover the phone and say, "Sadie, don't you dare steal her mac and cheese, darn it." His voice came through again. "I ended up taking the week off hoping to help her settle in. Took a vacation I hadn't had in years, so it was no big deal. I think it was the right thing to do. I almost got her to smile the other day. And I found someone to watch her for me next week, so that's handled. So far so good."

There. See. They're fine. No need to worry.

"Good. Great." She played with the cord on her phone. "Look. I know it's a big pain in the rear, but I'll need to check up on you from time to time. Once a child is in my care, I kind of have to keep tabs on them."

She heard a muffled sound that made her think he'd switched the phone to his other ear. "No, that's fine. I was actually thinking about you the other day."

Why did her lungs stop working for a second? "Oh?"

"Well, not you precisely. About you and what you guys do there. It seems crazy that you have such a shortage of foster parents when there are so many couples out there that can't have kids, so I thought maybe we should do something to help you out. You know. Have a fund-raiser or something. Help get the word out that there are kids in need. An awareness day or whatever. My aunt's a whiz at producing events. She puts on a big horse show every year, including an exhibitor party that would do Hollywood proud. If we held an event out here it would be a great way to inform the public of your needs."

He wanted to help.

She shouldn't be surprised. "I don't know." She took a deep breath. "I'd have to think about that for a bit."

"Sure, sure."

Who was she kidding? It was exactly what they needed. They didn't have the budget for television spots or radio ads like the private foster agencies did. It was all she could do to operate with what the state of California gave her, and yet this week alone they'd had three new kids come in, all from different families. One of them would ultimately be returned to Mom once she cleaned up her act, but there was still the issue of temporary foster care. What she wouldn't give for a dozen more like Maverick.

"Tell you what," he said. "Why don't you come on out to the ranch and we'll talk about it."

Out to the ranch?

How was it possible to want something and then also *not* want something? She had no idea why she always reacted to him in such a strange way whenever he was near. It was almost like she was afraid of him, and that was silly. She'd dealt with other good-looking foster dads in the past. This foster dad was a saint. And yet even just talking to him on the phone made her palms sweat. Why?

Whatever the reason, she wouldn't let it affect the future of Via Del Caballo Child Protective Services.

"I guess I could do that, especially if I combine it with a wellness check."

"Cool. Maybe today? I know that's short notice, but we're home, doing nothing, so it'd be a good time."

"Oh, well—"

"I can show you pictures of what we've done in the past. Heck, I can even show you the arena where we hold the big events. I can ask my aunt to come over. You can meet her and talk about what you need."

"Yeah, sure. But it'd have to be later."

"Great."

No, it wasn't great, she thought as she hung up. Not great at all because she'd never felt so anxious about seeing one of her foster dads. It didn't make any sense.

"You like this woman, don't you?"

His aunt Crystal stared at him like a surgeon would a broken arm, and he should know because his sister-in-law Ava was an orthopedic surgeon and he'd seen the way she used to look at his brother Carson's arm when in the hospital. Still, he tried not to squirm under the intensity of that gaze because his aunt could spot a fib a mile away. He'd once left the gate to the pasture wide open. A few dozen head of cattle had gotten out and destroyed a portion of the vineyard. His own mom had believed his lie, but not Aunt Crystal. Oh, no. She'd squeezed the truth out of him in no time flat.

"I like what she does for kids," he clarified.

They were sitting in his family room, his aunt on a couch his brother Carson had made out of oak and leather and metal buttons, although how the heck Carson had managed to do it, he had no idea. Maverick sat in a matching chair that he'd dubbed "the throne." It was huge and matched the couch except it had real cow hide hair instead of smooth leather. Crystal held Olivia on her knee, bouncing her up and down, trying to coax one of Olivia's rare smiles out of her. So far he'd managed to care for the little girl without killing her, but that was thanks in large part to his aunt, who Maverick now called his child-rearing consultant.

"Is she pretty?" Crystal asked, bouncing, bouncing, bouncing.

An image of Charlotte's smile came to mind. "I don't know, Aunt Crystal. She's always got her hair up, and she always wears these button-up shirts and stuff. Impossible to tell."

"Maverick Stewart Gillian." The bouncing stopped. Even Olivia seemed to sit up straighter, although that might be because of Charlotte's tone of voice. "I would hope I've taught you that beauty has nothing to do with a woman's hair or what's underneath her shirt."

Said one of the most beautiful women in Via Del Caballo. His aunt had been a rodeo queen in her youth and it was easy to understand why. Her blond hair had turned gray, but it'd been a platinum color that came directly from nature and not a bottle. Her blue eyes were still huge and set into a face unmarked by age.

"Don't listen to him, Olivia," she said in a singsong voice. "Your grandmother raised him better than that."

Thoughts of his mom had him staring at his hands. This whole week he'd missed her with a fierceness that struck him hard, more now than ever because he could have really used her guidance. He'd never been close to his dad, although not for lack of trying. Maverick wasn't big into rodeos like his older brothers were. Wasn't a favorite son like Flynn was, his oldest brother having inherited his dad's passion for breeding horses. But that was okay. His dad left him alone to run the ranch while most of the family was off showing horses or watching

Shane or Carson at a rodeo, and that was the way Maverick liked it.

"She's got a good heart," he admitted. "I mean, who wouldn't admire a woman who committed herself to helping needy kids?"

His aunt went back to bouncing. "I can't wait to meet her."

Less than an hour later she had her wish. A car pulled up to the front, and then a second later a door slammed, a reflection from the driver's side glass penetrating the big-pane window of his family room with a flash. He got up out of his chair, tensing for some reason, his aunt watching as he crossed the room to greet Charlotte at the door.

Sadie had greeted her first. Charlotte stopped in her tracks on the porch, staring down at the dog as if uncertain what to do.

"Just ignore her," he said.

She sidled around the canine, and he wondered if she was afraid of animals or something.

"I told you she's a sweetheart. You should see the way she's taken to Olivia. Sleeps at the foot of her crib every night."

"Oh, I'm sure she is. I'm just not used to dogs."

When she got closer he realized her brown eyes had flecks of green in them. Not really hazel. Still brown, but spotted by color. Pretty.

"Glad you could come out."

Sadie had clearly decided Charlotte needed investigating and followed at her heels. She'd gotten protective with Olivia, although at first his dog wasn't sure what to think about the tiny human living with them. Sadie had followed her around the house, but Maverick had a feeling his collie only did it because she thought the little girl might need to be herded out of trouble.

"Sadie, leave her alone."

Charlotte glanced back at his dog, and he wondered if she'd changed before coming over. He'd never seen her in boots and jeans before. No button-down blouse today, just a black T-shirt that clung to curves he hadn't even known existed, her hair loose around her shoulders.

"I thought I should change," she said, and he realized she must have caught the direction of his gaze and it had made her self-conscious. "You mentioned something about an arena."

"No, no. You look fine. I was just expecting the business you." His dog circled her feet and he sighed. "Sadie. Stop it."

The black-and-white dog glanced between the two of them, and Maverick would swear his canine friend waited for Charlotte to give her a command.

"Inside," he ordered. The dog obediently slipped through the door.

"Come on in."

"Thanks."

He caught a whiff of her when she passed. Lemons and vanilla. It was a smell that reminded him of his youth. Lemon cookies, he realized. His mom used to make them all the time. Funny how he just now remembered that.

"Aunt Crystal, this is Charlotte." He hung back while Charlotte entered the family room. "She's in charge of Via Del Caballo Child Protective Services."

His aunt smiled up at Charlotte with the warmth and friendliness that she was known for. "So nice to meet you, Charlotte. I'd shake your hand, but mine are a little full at the moment."

"That's okay." Charlotte crossed over to her, kneeling down in the same way she had that first day. "Hey there, young lady. How are you?"

Olivia had turned her head at the sound of the stranger's voice, her eyes widening a bit when she spotted Charlotte.

"Can I hold her?" Charlotte asked.

"Of course."

Charlotte held out her hands and smiled at Olivia in a way that made Maverick's whole body still. There were two sides of her, he thought. The shy, businesslike side of her, and the loving, warm side that she reserved for her kids.

"Oh, my goodness," she said. "You've gained weight." She touched her nose to Olivia's. "That's so wonderful."

"She actually eats like a horse," Maverick said. "And I should know. I'm a slave to her dietary needs."

"She's a darling little girl," Crystal said. "But I did want to ask you—is it normal for her not to talk? So far all she does is make noises. She'll reach for things. Point. That kind of stuff, but that's all."

"She said *mama* the first day we brought her home," Maverick said.

"Oh?" his aunt replied. "But not since."

Maverick shook his head. Charlotte was still smiling down at the little girl.

"More normal than you might think," she said. "Especially when a child has been neglected. They need human interaction to pick up on words, and I'm afraid Olivia has had precious little of that."

"Was it really that bad?" his aunt asked.

"Almost as bad as I've ever seen." Charlotte faced his aunt. "And I've seen some terrible stuff."

"Well, that's just tragic." Crystal met his gaze, sadness in her eyes. "Becca was a lovely girl. In fact, there was a time when I thought she and Maverick might work out."

"Aunt Crystal, no. It was never like that between us."

"Not for her lack of trying." Crystal shook her head. "That girl was in love with you for years, Maverick, but you never gave her the time of day."

"Not true."

Crystal just shook her head. "Men. Sometimes they're so blind to these things. But Maverick's not the type to lead a woman on. Becca might have thought she was in love with him at one time, but she got over it, and then she started hanging around with those Hamilton boys." She stood up, reaching out to swipe a lock of Olivia's hair off her face. "And that was the beginning of the end. So sad."

"I've heard stories like that before." Charlotte's smile turned sad. "It's a shame what drugs can do to someone."

"It is. Thank goodness she had the good sense to put Maverick down on that birth certificate—otherwise, who knows where her child would have ended up."

"Aunt Crystal, please. That wasn't exactly a nice thing to do."

"No, it was a sign of her desperation, Maverick. But it's all water under the bridge. We'll see Olivia wants for nothing while she's in our care."

Charlotte met his aunt's gaze. "I can tell you already are, and I can't thank you enough for that." She looked over at him, but it was from beneath her lashes. "Both of you. Olivia is truly lucky to have you."

"Any luck on finding her a permanent home?" Crystal asked.

"I'm afraid not. We're stretched so thin these days. One of our families has a daughter that's close to aging out, but it's not uncommon for kids to stay with their foster parents well beyond eighteen, so I'll have to wait and see."

"As long as it's a good home," Crystal said, her eyes softening. "Nothing but the best for that little girl."

"Of course," Charlotte said.

At last she looked him in the eyes, and he just sort of went "Oh" at what he saw in them. Gratitude. Approval. Respect, and something else, something he couldn't quite put his finger on, but that made him duck his own head and stuff his hands in his pockets.

Crystal held out her hand. "Here." She wiggled her fingers. "Let me take Olivia. Maverick wants to give you a tour."

"Aren't you going to come, too?" Maverick asked.

"Oh, goodness, no. Run along, you two." She took Olivia. "I'm going to spend some time with this little girl. When you come back from showing her around we can talk. In the meantime, have fun."

Chapter 9

Have fun? Charlotte thought. This crazy upside-down, inside-out feeling she had whenever Maverick was around was not fun. It was…troubling.

"Do you want to walk?" Maverick asked, turning outside the front door and telling Sadie to stay.

For some strange reason she wished the dog was going with them. Given how uncomfortable canines made her feel, she admitted it was a sign of desperation. Moral support, even the four-legged kind, was what she needed.

"Walk," she said, because she didn't want to be in a vehicle with him alone. She would feel too…too vulnerable.

"Come on. This way, then."

She walked alongside of him, his big shoulders so much higher than her own she found herself wondering how he found horses big enough to carry him. But it was his eyes that kept drawing her in, the softness in them, the kindness.

"I really appreciate—"

"My aunt thinks—"

They both stopped talking at the same time, and then, despite her discomfort, Charlotte smiled. The right side of his mouth lifted, too, and she heard a low rumble that she realized was the start of a laugh. She looked down at the ground, the cowboy boots she wore once a year—at the Via Del Caballo annual rodeo—scuffing the dirt road. She took a deep breath, focusing on their surroundings. She'd never seen a more glorious location in her life. The sun was still high enough in the late-afternoon sky that it lit up the trees around them, casting long shadows on the ground. This time of year, the grass was still green, a slight breeze catching the tops of the longer blades and causing them to dance.

"You go ahead," she said.

"I was just going to say my aunt thinks holding a fundraiser of some kind is a great idea. She said we could get media out to the ranch and invite some of our cutting horse friends and local families. The ones with the means to help out, if you know what I mean."

She nodded. "I'd have to look into whether we can take private donations. We may have to go the route of a media event. You know, invite the press so they can help spread the word about what our needs are, which is basically one thing—foster parents."

They lapsed into silence and she tried not to feel self-conscious as she walked alongside of him, but it proved to be impossible. The man seemed as large as a stuntman off a movie set. Never, not in all her life, had she had such a visceral reaction to a man. Usually men were

so far off her radar that when one of the girls in the office made a comment about a good-looking delivery guy
or foster father, she found herself taken aback. But with
Maverick, she finally understood what it was like to look
at a man and think, *Wow*.

"So, I saw on your form that Maverick's not your real
name. Why do they call you that, then?" she asked into
the silence that made her uncomfortable.

He smiled down at her, and she realized he wasn't
wearing a cowboy hat, and that his hair was shaggy
and nearly black and so thick it was no wonder his eyes
looked like those of an '80s rock star, all fake eyeliner
and dark lashes.

"My dad wanted to name me something hideous, and
to hear my mom tell it, they argued her entire pregnancy.
In the end, my dad got his way, but Mom was a huge fan
of the movie *Top Gun*, so she started calling me Maverick
just to get my dad's goat and it kind of stuck. The rest, as
they say, is history."

He lifted his hands. "And if you saw my real name,
then you know why I don't like it."

"I have seen it," she reminded him with a smile. "And
I agree. Fineus doesn't exactly seem like something to
call a cowboy."

"No, not really."

He laughed again, and she liked this newer, more relaxed Maverick. He'd calmed down. A week of parenting had calmed him down. This was the real Maverick.
A man of quiet confidence and compassion.

"I like Maverick better." His smile turned rueful.

He wasn't afraid of admitting how mortified he was
by his real name and she found that...surprising. In her

experience, men didn't like to admit a weakness, but this one clearly didn't mind.

"Looks like we'll have the barn to ourselves." He pointed down the road, and she caught a glimpse of the magnificent stable she'd passed each time she'd driven in. "Nobody parked out front."

"It looks like someone's home it's so pretty," she mused.

"It does, kind of. Never thought about it."

Because he was so used to the splendor of the place, he probably never saw it like everyone else did. The first time she'd seen it from a distance she'd thought that was exactly what it was—a home—but then she realized the big sandy area was an arena. It looked like it belonged next to a California mission with its Spanish tile roof, stucco exterior walls and an arched entry that gave her a glimpse of luxurious stall fronts inside. No horses peeked their heads out, but that was because wrought iron bars lined the tops of the wooden stall fronts and kept the horses inside the stall.

"You could film a movie here," she said.

They were on a slight rise, the vineyards spreading outward to her left, the grass-covered hills in the distance. Beautiful in a way that she'd never seen before.

"They actually have."

They had paused near the entrance. "So the arena is right through there." He motioned toward the rear entrance and the sandy area out past the barn's sliding wooden doors.

"What we've done in the past is covered the arena with a giant tent, the kind they use for weddings, only bigger, and if you're worried about the footing, don't be. We wet the sand down beneath it and then roll it so that it forms a kind of hardpan. The arena's big enough that you can seat a hundred and fifty people pretty easily at what my aunt calls rounds—they're just round tables. That's if we decide to do a sit-down dinner. We could always just do cocktails. My sister's boss did a huge grand opening celebration in his arena, although his place is covered, but it's definitely doable. We'd just need to decide what type of event."

It could work. She didn't have any doubt about that.

"Maverick, I can't afford to pay for any of this. You know that, don't you?"

They stood in the shade of the barn, his blue eyes searching her own. "We figured as much, but you don't need to worry about that. We'll foot the bill."

She spotted a horse inside a stall, walked forward. The animal inside was a gorgeous red color, her mane long and silky and ink black.

"That's my niece's horse, Snazzy. She shows her at cutting competitions."

Charlotte shook her head. What would it be like to grow up in a place like this? she wondered. To have horses and siblings and a beautiful home to live in. To wake up every day and be able to walk among such beauty. It only solidified her determination to convince Maverick to take Olivia permanently. What a lucky little girl she would be.

"Some of our kids would go nuts out here." She held out her hand. The horse inside the stall walked forward and reached for the bars with her nose, but when she went to pet the animal, it shied away.

"Like this," he said, coming forward.

Everything inside her froze when he touched her, and not because she feared him like she had other men in her past. No. This was different. This was like that moment when she'd taken the kids to an amusement park and they'd ridden that huge roller coaster, and she'd sat in the front and had a perfect view of that first, terrifying drop. She'd been so afraid and excited all at the same time.

She tried to snatch her hand away and glanced up at him, noting the stubble on his jawline and the way he smelled and that the veins on his biceps stood out beneath the sleeves of his polo shirt in the way of men who were physically fit.

"Don't be afraid."

"I'm not afraid," she lied.

He wouldn't let her go. "Just flatten your hand." He gently tugged on her fingers, and his touch was so soothing and so gentle that she told herself not to move. She didn't want him touching her, but *not* for the reasons she usually rejected a man's touch. Oh, no. When Maverick clasped her fingers, it was like landing on a different planet, overwhelming and exhilarating and strange.

The horse came forward again. Its breath touched her first, and then its nose, the hair so soft and the way the upper lip moved—like an elephant's—that she forgot for a second that a man held her hand.

"There," he said softly. "See."

He let her go. She almost collapsed against the front of the stall.

"A horse's touch can soothe the soul."

She glanced up at him sharply, wondering if he'd sensed her tension, but he was staring at the horse. He had a whimsical smile on his face. He seemed to gather himself, straightened a bit and glanced back down at her.

"That's what my mom always said."

"You were close to her."

She didn't mean it as a question. She'd been desperate to distract herself from the way being so near to him made her feel. But she'd stared into enough eyes over the years to know that she'd hit a nerve.

"Super close."

Her breath hitched for a moment. She saw sadness in his eyes, and as it always did, it evoked an urge to comfort him, but she couldn't do that.

"You were lucky."

Something about her words had caught his attention because he cocked his head like a bird that had heard the cry of a friend.

"What about you? Were you close to your parents?"

She flinched, peered back at the horse and hoped he hadn't seen the way she'd reacted.

"No."

Not to any of her so-called parents, but the last one, that one had been the worst—well, the father and his biological son.

She didn't want to think about it, much less talk about it, and so she said, "We have a little boy in foster care right now who would love to visit your ranch."

He peered down at her and she knew—she just knew—that he'd seen her reaction, and more, that he'd somehow figured out what she'd been through. That he'd gleaned the terrible truth she hid from most people. She thought he might press the issue, but he didn't and, in hindsight, she shouldn't be surprised. If she'd learned anything about the man, it was that he understood the complexities of the human heart, and that kindness would always keep him quiet if the situation warranted.

"It's strange how some kids are born horse crazy," he said.

It was an obvious change of subject on his part and she was grateful.

"Yes, it is, Fineus."

He frowned down at her, but it was a playful look, one that conveyed his understanding of her need to lighten the mood.

"Careful now," he said.

"I think I should call you that all the time."

"Not if you want to remain friends."

Friends? She supposed they were turning into that. And it wasn't like her to tease a man, and the thought sobered her as they lapsed into silence.

"You should bring that little boy out here," he said a moment later.

She felt her brows lift in surprise. "Oh, no, I couldn't, and I didn't mean to infer—"

"Hup. Hup." He lifted his hands, and she could see the thoughtful consideration in his eyes. "I'm going somewhere with this. Maybe that's the direction we should go in for this event. We could invite some of your foster families to come out. See if they'd share their experience with the people who attend, have them talk about what it's like to give a home to children like Olivia."

"But I—"

"No, no. Promise me you'll think about it. It could really have an impact on people. And knowing my aunt, she'll invite a ton of people to the benefit or gala or whatever we end up calling it, all of them potential new foster parents, not to mention the media exposure would be great. Nothing like free drinks to bring out the press."

He had a point, but it meant she'd have to see more of him, and he made her feel so off balance and strange that she didn't want that. She wanted to go hide in a hole, or maybe her office, just do her job and leave and forget about the hidden splendor of Gillian Ranch.

"I don't know what to say." She went back to staring at the horse because staring into his eyes made her feel even more odd.

"Say you'll do it."

She took a deep breath. She'd be a fool to say no.

"Okay."

"You'll do it?"

"I will."

He smiled and she felt such a sudden burst of hero worship that it darn near clogged her throat. She swallowed, hard.

"Great," he said.

Great for the kids. Not for her.

Chapter 10

"So that was Charlotte," his aunt said the moment the two of them were alone.

He almost went back outside where he'd just been seeing Charlotte off. He recognized the opening volley of a coming inquisition. Just what he needed.

"Yes, that was Charlotte," he said, glancing over at Olivia, who sat in the family room on a blanket playing with the plastic blocks his aunt had bought her. "You want me to cook you some dinner? I heard Uncle Bob is off picking up some cattle."

"No, that's okay." He walked into the kitchen and heard his aunt stand up and follow him. "I have about a million things to do at home."

If he were honest, he was almost glad she didn't want to stay. But he should have known he wouldn't escape that easily. She stopped in the entry to his kitchen just off the front foyer, and Maverick kept an eye on Olivia through the doorway. She seemed perfectly content to sit on the floor.

"So, did she agree to let us help her?" she asked, leaning against the door.

"She did."

"Good." His aunt stayed in the doorway. He turned to grab a pot so he could start boiling water for noodles. He'd probably gained ten pounds since Olivia had come to live with him. He used to skip dinner a lot, but now all he seemed to do was cook pasta. The kid couldn't get enough of it.

"She seems nice."

"She is."

"And way prettier than I expected."

He said nothing.

"And so good with kids," she added.

He set the pot on the stove, turned the switch and, because he no longer had anything else to distract him, faced his aunt, although he refused to comment.

"I wonder why some man hasn't snapped her up," she said.

Why she'd shrunk away from him when he'd reached for her hand. Abuse? he wondered. The thought upset him.

"No comment, huh?"

It took him a moment to remember his aunt's question. From the family room Olivia let out a squeal that had them both turning in her direction. Sadie had walked over to her and, evidently, had sat down on her blocks.

"No," the little girl said, wagging a finger.

They both froze.

Olivia tottered to her feet, her hands moving to Sadie's

face, her tiny hands pushing against her snout so hard that the skin along the gum line pushed up, revealing Sadie's teeth. Sadie didn't move.

"No," Olivia said again.

"Well, I'll be," Crystal murmured. "She picked up on one word, at least."

"Sadie, come."

The dog leaped to her feet, pushing Olivia off balance. She landed on her rear so hard she started to cry.

"Sadie," Maverick scolded.

"Come here, darling," said his aunt at the same time.

"No, I'll get her," Maverick said, giving his dog the stink eye when she crossed to his side. "Bad dog," he told the collie, but inside his heart sang. Olivia had said something. Granted, it was only one word, but it was a start.

"It's okay," he said, scooping her up. She cried like someone had taken the blocks and burned them in front of her, and he pulled her up to him. When her tiny arms wrapped around him, and when she burrowed her head into the crook of his neck, his throat thickened like someone had poured cement down it, and suddenly it was hard to breathe.

"Aw, look at her cuddle," Crystal said.

When he met his aunt's gaze, her own lids were suspiciously moist. "I always thought you'd make a great dad."

"I'm not her dad," he said over the muffled sound of Olivia's tears.

"But you could be. Permanently."

"Aunt Crystal, no. This is only temporary, remember?"

"So you'd let her go to strangers?"

He hadn't thought about it. And now he didn't want to think about it, so he focused on soothing the little girl.

"Come on, Sadie. Outside," Crystal said. "You've offended that poor child's dignity. Go hide until she calms down."

The front door opened and closed, and when his aunt came back she stared at him with a knowing look in her eyes.

"Face it, Maverick, that little girl is going to burrow herself straight into your heart, and when the time comes to give her up, you're going to feel like you're losing a limb."

Olivia had calmed down, her sobbing having turned to snuffles. She'd relaxed in his arms and he knew that his aunt was right. He'd hate it.

"Whatever my feelings are when the time comes, she deserves two loving parents."

"Like you had?"

He searched for a hidden meaning behind his aunt's words and found none. Her blue eyes considered him carefully, but that was all. Had she known about the tension in the house before his mom's death?

"Like *all* kids should have."

A brow lifted. "These days lots of people raise kids on their own."

"Yeah, but not me."

Her lips pressed together. "Old-fashioned."

"Maybe."

Or maybe he'd never really thought about it. He'd never been close to proposing to someone, never thought about a family. It had seemed too far off in the distance, but maybe it was closer than he'd thought.

"Do you mind putting some noodles in that water there?" he asked his aunt.

"You should put her in the swing. She looks ready to go to sleep."

He took a peek at her, gray eyes heavy-lidded, but they met his own, and when they did he felt the same kind of sensation as he did when he looked into the eyes of his brother's kids. Strange.

"You want to swing while Daddy—" He stopped. "While I cook dinner."

After he'd settled her in the chair he turned back to his aunt.

"I caught that," she said.

"Nothing to it, Auntie."

"Just like there's nothing to the way you look at that woman."

"Aunt Crystal—"

"No, no." She lifted her hand. "I'm going to leave you to it. Just ask yourself one question. Why are you going to so much trouble if you don't like her at least a little bit?"

"I like her." He shook his head. Earlier he'd been pretty certain they'd end up as friends. "But it's not the kind of like that will ever turn into anything. I also feel sorry for her because she works so hard."

She was the type of person who threw her whole heart into helping kids. He admired that about her, that was all.

His aunt had come forward, reaching up to kiss him on the cheek before she said, "Keep telling yourself that."

A week later Charlotte stared at the words in front of her for a full thirty seconds.

Conclusion: Maverick Gillian is excluded as the father of Olivia Gillian.

There it was in black and white, just as he'd said. He wasn't the baby's father, and so unless by some miracle someone walked into her office and admitted to being Olivia's father, the little girl would now become a ward of the state of California. And while she wasn't all that surprised, it was still a disappointment, and she had to sit there and analyze why.

She'd been hoping Olivia would stay with Maverick.

But if he'd been lying, that would have changed her opinion of him, and not for the better, and that had to be part of the conflicting emotions she felt, too. The man was a saint. She supposed she'd been hoping to find a chink in his armor.

Why?

He was a kind, caring man who'd taken in a little girl for no other reason other than he felt he owed it to her mom.

What a testament to his character.

She pushed back from her desk, spinning around so she could see out the front. Outside had dawned a gorgeous day. The mountains in the distance, the ones that separated their small town from the coast, were covered in green. Cars drove by and she wished she could be like the drivers inside, oblivious to the darker side of life. So many kids. So few qualified people to take care of them. But the Gillians wanted to help her with that, and she wasn't too proud to accept that help even if it meant working with a man who made her question her vow to steer clear of the opposite sex.

Her phone pinged again. She turned around to face it.

My aunt was wondering if you'd like to join us for family dinner at her place on Sunday night to discuss the upcoming event?

Speak of the devil.

She thought about ignoring the text, and she didn't want to think about why. But she couldn't do that. Family dinner would give her a chance to meet the people closest to Maverick. That was part of her job, to follow up with family members on Olivia's care.

Sure. What time?

He texted a time and directions to his aunt's house, which appeared to be one of the homes on the hill behind the stables she'd visited. She texted back confirmation that she'd be there, but then her gaze caught on the document in front of her. She was tempted to raise the issue with him, but she knew he'd receive a copy, too. This wasn't television. There would be no big, dramatic courtroom reveal about Olivia's parentage. He would still need to appear in front of a judge to make things official, but that was the extent of his obligation. He owed them nothing.

But he'd bend over backward for Olivia. He was that kind of man.

Chapter 11

That Sunday, as Charlotte drove out to the Gillian Ranch, she wondered at the way her hands shook and her belly tightened.

She passed between acres and acres of pasture, the valley opening up in front of her revealing the vineyards on both sides of the road and then, beyond that, the stables to her right and the homes up on the hills behind them. He'd told her his father had the place on the right and so she kept to the left, cresting a small hill and then dipping into another small valley before she began to climb up another hill. When she reached the top, the trees opened up and a single-story Spanish-style home sprawled out in front of her, one with thick, square columns along the front and large windows whose panes of glass were divided by wood frames. Parked outside were a number of vehicles, mostly trucks, all of them probably at least a dozen years newer than her own beat-up old Ford car. She spent her money on things she probably shouldn't pay for—like diapers and baby formula and clothing, things the state paid for, too, but there never seemed to be enough.

"Alrighty." The word sounded like a sigh even to her own ears, and she clutched the steering wheel for a moment before taking a deep breath and slipping into the warm spring air.

She'd had no idea just how high she'd climbed until she caught a view of the valley out behind the house. Off in the distance, to her left, she could see Maverick's father's home; it was lower and partially shielded by trees. Down below her the vineyard looked like a bumpy lawn. The leaves were a vivid green compared to the grass-covered pastures that surrounded it, the oak trees that dotted the horizon nearly a gunmetal gray. It was like a giant puzzle from her vantage point, a key-shaped vineyard, a rectangular pasture, the zigzag lines of rock wall, all that open space shaded in different greens.

"There she is," said Crystal, the woman she'd met with at Maverick's home, and in her arms was Olivia, the little girl having put on so much weight in such a short amount of time that Charlotte barely recognized her. "Say hello, Olivia."

The little girl eyed her curiously, but there was something different about her eyes, and it took her a moment to pinpoint what it was.

Happy.

The eyes were no longer dull and lifeless. Now they seemed lit up from inside, as a world of curiosities had presented themselves and she couldn't wait to get her hands on it all.

It made her want to cry.

"Say hi," Crystal repeated.

The little girl lifted a hand and then said as clear as day, "Hello."

This…this was why she did what she did for a living, why she made so many sacrifices, the reason she'd dedicated her life to helping children.

"Well, hello," Charlotte said right back, closing the distance between them. "May I hold her?"

"Of course," Crystal said. "But be careful. She's a wiggle worm these days. She's learned how to run, or maybe she always knew, but she refuses to slow down now."

Charlotte wondered if Olivia recognized the woman who'd found her amid such squalor, if maybe she would associate her presence with her past. It happened sometimes. But the little girl had clearly put the past behind her because she smiled and willingly sank into her arms.

"Hi, sweetie," she said softly. "How are you?"

"Come on in," Crystal said.

She was grateful for Olivia's presence when she walked into a home as spacious and beautiful as she'd imagined—like the lobby of an upscale hotel with its tile floors and lush plants that crouched in corners. The little girl was like a shield that she held tight because Maverick's family wasn't just big, it was huge—at least half-a-dozen pairs of eyes turned toward her when she walked in. A massive kitchen opened up to her left, a waist-high island in the middle where two dark-haired men sat.

"Everyone, this is Charlotte. She's the social worker we were telling you all about."

There was a chorus of hellos before Crystal turned back to her, long gray hair falling over one shoulder. She pointed to the family room that opened up in front of them. "So, sitting on the couch is my husband, Bob, and next to him is my niece, Jayden, and her daughter, Paisley. On the couch opposite her is her husband, Colby. And next to him is my nephew Carson. His wife, Ava, is working, but his daughter, Bella, is around here somewhere."

"She's down at the barn," said Carson. "Flynn will be bringing her up later."

"Well, that figures," said Crystal with a smile. "Flynn is another nephew of mine. And over there in the kitchen are two of my sons."

She pointed to the kitchen that looked like it belonged in a magazine with its granite countertops and stainless steel appliances. "That's Tyler there on the right with the cowboy hat on. And opposite him is Terrence. And of course, you know Maverick there by the fridge."

Her body reacted in a weird way when she met his gaze, not that he seemed to notice. She clutched Olivia even closer. The little girl had spotted him, though, and leaned toward him, arms outstretched.

"Want."

"You want something to drink?" he asked the little girl, smiling at her. "What about you? You want something?"

"Uh, sure." It seemed as if all the moisture in her mouth had gone away. He wore a blue-checkered shirt that matched the color of his eyes and jeans cinched tight by a leather belt, a gold-and-silver buckle catching the light. "Water."

"Nice to meet you," said the one named Tyler.

"Same," said Terrence, his blue eyes catching on the little girl. "Hey, sweetheart."

"Here." Maverick brought Olivia a sippy cup, but she batted it away.

"Want." She held out her arms and it was clear what she wanted. Maverick.

"Here, let me take her," said his aunt.

No. She didn't want to give Olivia up.

"Come to auntie, sweet pea." Crystal smiled at her. "If I don't get her out of here soon, she'll have a full-on meltdown. The poor thing is head over heels for my nephew, but I'm not surprised. He spoils her rotten."

Maverick's brows lifted beneath a black cowboy hat. "I do not."

"You do, too," Crystal said, taking Olivia from her.

Charlotte had never felt more uncomfortable in her life. The two good-looking men at the counter went back to talking about grapes and barrels and something else. Someone laughed in the family room, Jayden's husband. She'd never been in the presence of such a huge family in her life. The Gillian men weren't like ordinary men. Each of them was tall and broad shouldered and so tan you could tell they spent their lives out of doors. For the first time she understood the appeal of cowboys. They seemed to ooze raw masculinity.

"Here." Maverick smiled as he handed her a bottled water. She took it, twisting off the lid and taking a sip all the while wondering if there was a way to slip outside. Even though the house was huge, it felt crowded inside.

"Want!" Olivia cried, the word startling everyone in the house into silence.

"See," Crystal called. "This is what happens when you spoil a child. I swear, Maverick. You're going to turn her into a daddy's girl if you're not careful."

Charlotte was staring right at him, and so she saw the way his eyes flickered and the way his mouth flinched.

She knew the word *daddy* had hit a nerve. When their gazes connected, he smiled at her sheepishly.

"I guess I should go hide."

"Actually, I was kind of hoping we could talk privately?"

He nodded. "Sure." He motioned for her to follow. "Guys, we're going to the lookout. Be back."

"Good," said his aunt. "Take your time. Maybe I can get her put down for a nap with you out of the way."

She would never have expected Olivia to take to Maverick like she had. It made her wonder why it surprised her so much. Probably because he'd been so reluctant to take her at first and Olivia had been so clearly traumatized by her past. But maybe that was why the little girl had become so attached. He was probably the first person to shower her with love, and the thought made her throat thicken all over again.

"This way." He headed past the parked vehicles and toward a path off to their left, one that led up a slight incline. They faced west, the hill the home sat upon eclipsed by a slightly bigger one behind it. Trees dotted the hillside on their left and right, the path she followed worn down by countless feet. She could see the imprint of boot heels in the dirt.

"So, does the whole family work the ranch?" she asked.

He tucked his hands in his pockets as he walked. He smelled like leather and talcum powder, and it made her blush that she'd even noticed it.

"Yep, my siblings work for the ranch and my cousins the vineyard. Everyone but my sister."

"Oh?" She took another swig of her water. "Ranch life not for her?"

"I wouldn't say that." He kicked a rock, the thing bouncing ahead of them. "Jayden was never into working cattle or growing grapes. She loves horses, but then she had a baby right out of high school and it was this whole big deal." He stared at the dirt path in front of them. "Some low-life scumbag knocked her up, and it upset my dad enough that he kicked her off the ranch."

"Ouch."

"I know, but that was right around the time my mom died. Tough time for us all. I don't think my dad was in his right mind. But then he had heart problems and it sort of changed his whole outlook, I think."

"So they patched things up?"

"Yup. It's not often Reese Gillian admits he's wrong, but he did last year. By then Paisley was two years old."

A massive oak tree loomed ahead, one with branches that hung heavy with age, the tips of the leaves touching the ground. It was so huge it had to have been growing in that spot forever. Valley oaks, they were called—the Spanish had loved them for the shade they provided. It sat atop the hill like the crown jewel of the ranch.

"My sister met a man where she works. She married him earlier this year."

"Do they live on the ranch, too?"

"No-ho-ho-ho." He was smiling. "She still stubbornly refuses to work here even though my dad told her she could start her own therapy program at the ranch. That's what she does for a living, hippotherapy."

"That's horse therapy, right? For people with PTSD and stuff?" she asked.

They'd reached the tree, its shade providing welcome relief from the sun, and—oh, boy—the vista in front of her was a sight to see.

"Wow," she said.

He perched on the corner of the picnic table, leaning back and staring out at the view below them. "Something else, right?"

From atop the hill she could see Via Del Caballo in the distance, the buildings and streets patches of gray set in the middle of green grassland. The Gillians' property line could be seen, too, ducking in and out from between the hills, and she realized they owned far more land than she'd thought. The rock wall that encircled the property went on for miles and miles.

"How much land do you guys own?"

"Enough that caring for it is a full-time job. And, yeah, hippotherapy is done with horses. My sister works with disabled vets at Dark Horse Ranch right down the road."

She sat down next to him on the top of the picnic table, resting her feet on the bench that peeked out from beneath it, staring down at the patches of green and brown beneath her and marveling.

"I've always wondered if it really works," she said.

"You should talk to my sister about it. She swears by it. I'd bet her program would be great for troubled kids, too."

"Oh?"

"Horses have an amazing effect on people."

"Do they?"

Blue eyes the color of the ocean stared back at her. "I think it'd work wonders with some of your kids."

She swallowed, looked away. Now that she was faced with actually posing the question she'd come out here to ask, it seemed like such a far-fetched idea.

"I actually have another favor to ask."

"Shoot."

She took a deep breath. When in doubt, dive right in. "I was wondering if you'd like to take Olivia permanently."

He drew back in surprise, but then his face softened as he stared into the distance. "To tell you the truth, Charlotte, I've been kind of wondering about that myself."

Her heart stopped beating in her chest. She couldn't stop from touching him. "Oh, Maverick, if you did that…"

She couldn't speak over the emotions just the thought of it did to her insides. She'd never, not ever, felt the urge to kiss a man, but she did right then, and it made her turn away, stare at her hands.

"I think if you did that Olivia would be one very lucky little girl."

"Not sure how I'll manage it, but what parent does, huh?"

"You're so right. No one ever really knows what they're in for, but somehow they always manage it."

"And I'm already doing a good job. I think."

She pulled her hand back, but only because she suddenly realized she'd kept it there and that she'd wanted to clasp his hand and she shouldn't do that. She had to ball her hand into a fist.

"You're doing a great job."

He smiled. "Thanks." Then his smile faded, the flicker of emotions on his face telling her he grappled with what he'd just offered.

"When would I have to let you know if that's what I decide to do?"

Her hands were clenched so tight she felt her nails digging into her palms. "By the first court date, when the judge officially rules on her parentage." She swung toward him again, having forgotten about the paperwork she'd received. "You did get a copy of the DNA results, didn't you?"

He smiled sheepishly. "I did. Not that I didn't know already, but it was good to see it there in writing."

"I'm sorry I ever doubted you."

He looked into her eyes. "I'm not surprised you did." His smile turned rueful. "In your line of work, I'm sure men and women lie all the time."

She nodded. "They do."

"I hope you decide to do it, Maverick. I really do."

Something changed in the air, something that made her heart beat faster as he stared down at her. A warmth began to build, and a tingling in her limbs and extremities made her breath catch. She saw his gaze drop to her lips, just for a heartbeat but long enough that they warmed in anticipation of something that had her looking away again, and that made her fingers clench even more and had her insides doing cartwheels.

"Why do you do that?" he asked softly.

"What?"

"Look away from me all the time."

She met his gaze square on then. "I don't."

He smiled softly, and the cartwheels inside her turned into a free fall that made her want to do exactly what he accused her of. He was right. She had a hard time holding his gaze.

"Are you afraid of me?"

The question was so on point, so close to the truth that she held on to her obstinacy with both hands. But she wasn't afraid of him.

"No," she answered honestly.

She was afraid of herself.

Chapter 12

She reminded him of the kittens that had been born in the barn. One wrong move and they'd dart away.

"What happened to you to make you so shy?" he asked.

"I'm not shy."

Maybe he'd used the wrong word, he thought, pulling his gaze away and staring out at the view that he'd always taken for granted. Sure, he recognized its beauty, but it was in the same way one would admire a painting one passed in a hallway every day of their life. It was just there.

"You're so committed to kids, but you don't have any kids of your own," he said.

"I don't need kids of my own. I have dozens already."

"But don't you want a family? Your own family?" Her eyes were cast down again, and he knew he'd struck a nerve somehow.

"My work is my family."

She really was a beauty, he thought, her skin as smooth as his favorite silk shirt. It glowed as if a professional photographer had chosen the lighting. And her eyes. They were brown, but earlier he'd spotted bits of green in them, and her lashes were so long they were like dark webs against her cheeks. But in the depths of her gaze he spotted an insecurity that belied the confidence she tried to exude.

"Whoever he was, he really did a number on you."

"Excuse me?"

Her brows had lifted, and she leaned away from him in a way meant to stop him from questioning her further.

"We're not all bad, you know."

Her chin flicked up as if he'd challenged her sanity. "My dedication to kids has nothing to do with a broken heart, if that's what you're thinking."

She'd left her hair down, a lock of it blowing across her face. He was tempted to tuck it behind her ear, a gesture he knew she wouldn't welcome.

"You were a foster child, weren't you?"

Another bull's-eye. Her mouth flattened, eyes narrowing. She wanted to look away. He could tell by the way her chin trembled as she forced herself to face him head-on. His estimation of her went up another notch.

"And it wasn't a happy home, was it?"

"We should be getting back."

She started to stand. He clasped her hand. When she tried to pull away, he held on to her, like it was a lead rope and an unbroken mare on the end. Her eyes grew big.

Fear.

He let go of her hand. "I'm sorry."

Her chin trembled, and it felt like his stomach rolled over in his belly. It started a chain reaction, his throat thickening and gut kicking. She'd been abused. Badly.

"I'm going back." She turned away, footfalls firm, her head held high in the manner of someone who faced inner demons every day…and had learned to coexist with them. He recognized that look. It was the same one he'd seen on the wounded veterans his sister worked with at Dark Horse Ranch.

Pride held her shoulders square as she walked away. He let her go, wanting to touch her so badly his hands literally ached, fingers clenching. But he didn't want to push her, didn't want to make her even more afraid. He gave her space, waited a few seconds before setting off after her. When he came up alongside of her, he tucked his hands into his pockets. All he'd done was try to hold on to her hand and it'd scared her to death.

"I'm sorry," he said again.

"It's okay."

No, it wasn't. Her eyes had lost their shine.

"It was nothing," she added.

It really was nothing, but it was something to her. "Mind if I walk back with you?"

She shrugged, and he knew she struggled to compose herself. It made him feel like even more of a chump.

"I'll talk to my family this week about Olivia." He kept his eyes straight ahead. "I'll let you know what I decide."

He could tell she was grateful for the change of subject, or maybe it was the reminder of what he proposed to do, but either way, out of the corner of his eye, he saw her shoulders soften.

"Thank you," she said.

She took a deep breath, slowly gained control of herself. He'd done this to her, all with a mere touch. He couldn't begin to imagine what she'd been through to make her so afraid.

"The sooner you decide if you're keeping Olivia, the better," she said. "It will make things easier if we can start the process next week, when you're in court."

"I'll let you know before then."

She glanced up at him. It was as if she'd grabbed on to her strength with both hands. "Thank you, *Mav*."

He drew back in surprise. "You've seen the movie."

"Of course. Even caught it on television the other day."

She teased him. It was an effort to set him at ease, to tell him without words that she wasn't holding a grudge. He wanted to kiss her.

"It's a good movie."

She nodded. "If you're into shoot-'em-ups."

They walked in silence for a few more steps.

"You know the minute we get back my aunt is going to pounce on you about this benefit thing. Once she gets started there's no stopping her. She'll have a million questions for you."

"I really appreciate her willingness to help."

"I was thinking she's probably going to keep you busy with meetings and whatnot. So maybe you could bring that little boy out with you the next time you're here. You know, the one you mentioned that would love to visit our ranch."

"William."

"We can ask Jayden if she's willing to work with him. She's good with kids. And if it works out, maybe we can do something on a regular basis. You know, have a day at the ranch once a month."

She glanced up at him. "You'd be willing to do that?"

He stopped. "I just want to help."

Help you, he silently told her. Help her and the kids. That was what he wanted. So much it was almost a pain in his heart. That and kiss her, although he didn't understand why. She didn't like him touching her, much less kissing her, and yet he wanted to do both right at that moment.

"I'll see if I can arrange it."

When they made it back to the house, his aunt took her hand and led her away, calling over her shoulder that Olivia had fallen asleep in her arms, not surprising since she always went to bed early, so he watched Charlotte from afar.

Damaged and dedicated to her job. That was his assessment. Someone who would never settle down and marry.

So what? he told himself.

It was none of his business what she wanted to do in her future. He would just be her friend. He had a feeling she needed a few of those.

She couldn't sleep that night. She kept reliving what had happened, wondering what she could have done differently. All he'd done was hold her hand. He'd done that once before. Sure, he'd held on to her for longer than she wanted, but he'd immediately let go. It wasn't like…

She shook her head.

It'd been years and still she had to deal with the scars Rodney had left behind. That was why she'd always stayed away from men, she thought, thrusting a pillow over her head. Messed up. She didn't need to bring that kind of messiness into someone else's life, even someone as wonderful as Maverick. Which was why she started to cry. Good old-fashioned self-pity. He was a good man. A man with integrity and kindness and a moral compass that would never steer him wrong. Yet, still, his touch had frightened her.

It was a restless night. She woke up the next day and pulled the covers over her head, wishing with all her heart she could just roll over and go back to sleep. But she couldn't. She had the kids to think about.

"Good morning," Susan chirped a couple of hours later as Charlotte used her rear end to push open the front door. Her hands were full of the paperwork Crystal had handed her last night. "How'd your meeting go with the Gillians?"

"Good."

The whole dinner had been wonderful. She'd spoken to Jayden, Maverick's sister, fascinated by her tales of working with veterans and, yes, maybe a little bit jealous when she told the story of how she'd met her husband. Maverick had kept his distance and that made her feel terrible. He'd done nothing wrong, and yet clearly he felt bad about what had happened.

She'd walked away from the place thinking there could be no nicer family in all of Via Del Caballo. And that her life would have been so much different if she'd grown up surrounded by a family like Maverick's.

"So, is it a go, then? Are we doing this?" Susan asked.

"I think so, but I still need to hear back from the higher-ups."

"Speaking of that, Mr. Rocha called you." Susan thrust a tiny slip of paper across her desk. "He said he has no problem with your doing a media event. He thinks it's a great way to help generate publicity about our need for foster parents."

She couldn't deny the relief she felt. "Terrific. One less thing to worry about."

"So exciting."

It was. The high point of her evening had been talking to Crystal and listening to all the amazing ideas she had. There was even talk of a celebrity or two making an appearance. Some friend of a friend knew Rand Jefferson, the action-hero star. If everything went off without a hitch, there might even be the possibility of national media attention, and that would be, well, just amazing.

"I'll let the Gillians know the good news."

She had only taken two steps when they both heard the front door open. She turned in time to spot a huge bouquet of roses walking toward her. A moment later a face peeked around the edge of the red blooms.

Maverick.

"I caught you." He shifted the flowers off to his left. "I was worried you wouldn't be here."

"Are you kidding?" Susan said. "She's going to drop dead at her desk and then we'll have the funeral here."

She shot Susan a look of admonishment before turning back to Maverick, and the emotions he roused as she stood there gawking at those flowers, well, she couldn't put a name to them all. She knew, of course, that they were a peace offering. And the fact that it wasn't his fault, well, it made her feel terrible all over again.

"They're beautiful, Maverick."

"Oh, they're not for you." He hugged the flowers closer to him. "They're for my aunt. As a thanks for watching Olivia for me this morning. I just brought them inside so they wouldn't wilt from the heat."

She leaned back in surprise, but then he smiled and she knew he was messing with her.

"Good one, Mav."

He laughed. She found herself on the verge of laughter, too, and wanting to move toward him, to touch him and tell him how grateful she was for his kindness and understanding. Only he could bring her to the verge of laughter when all she'd wanted to do was run and hide.

"Here," he said, coming forward.

"Thank you." She clutched her message slips, took the flowers, immediately burying her nose in their huge blooms, inhaling their sweet scent.

Flowers. Her first. Ever.

"Actually, do you have a second?"

She'd be the world's most ungracious flower recipient if she told him no. "Sure. Come on in."

Susan had the strangest expression on her face as she walked by. Sort of a cross between surprise and approval and maybe even a little envy.

It's not what you think, she tried to tell the woman with her eyes. Susan responded with a silent *sure it isn't* wink right back.

She set the flowers down on the corner of her desk as she walked by. Braced herself as she turned to face him without sitting down. Progress, she realized. She didn't feel the need to hide behind her desk.

"I just wanted to say that if I'd known you were...that if you didn't like..." He was clearly at a loss for words, and she watched as he took a deep breath and said in a rush, "I'm sorry if I crossed some kind of invisible line last night."

She'd known he would say something like that. Of

course he would. He was Maverick, the kindest man she'd ever met.

"It's not your fault." His expression was one of self-reproach. "Really, it's not."

"Do you mind if I ask…? I mean, you don't have to answer. You can tell me to buzz off. I would totally understand. But I presume something happened when you were in foster care? Is that it?"

She swallowed, opened her mouth to say something pithy, something that would work as a brush-off, but the look in his eyes dared her to be honest. No. Maybe not dared. More like *encouraged*, and she figured she owed him at least a little bit of the truth.

"I had a foster brother. He was…" She had a hard time with words, too. "Not nice to me. And my foster parents were blind. The dad, he…" Even now she had a hard time saying it. "He didn't believe me when I told him what he'd done. He believed the boy."

There was so much more to it than that, but there were some things she didn't think she would ever share with anyone, not even someone like Maverick.

He hadn't said anything.

"Anyway," she said into the silence. "It's not even that uncommon a tale." She placed her palms on her desk. "And part of the reason why I do what I do for a living."

He continued to stare. She continued to grow more and more uncomfortable.

"Why do I get the feeling there's more to the story than what you're telling me?"

Because he was astute. And sharp-eyed. And the kind of man who could read between the lines.

"It's in my past, Maverick, and I prefer not to dwell on it."

It was the period on the end of the paragraph about her life. She didn't want to talk about it anymore and he seemed to take the hint.

"Whoever he was, he should be horsewhipped."

She'd be the first in line if that ever happened. But all she did was move around behind her desk, taking a seat, hoping he'd do the same thing, too.

"So I heard from my boss." *Please go along with the change of subject.* "Left me a message. Said we're good for a major media event."

He nodded and she realized he wasn't wearing a cowboy hat, and that had left the ends of his hair curling gently around his neck. She wondered if it was soft, but then her face filled with heat at the boldness of such a thought.

"And I think I'll bring William out to the ranch next week. He's been going through a tough time. Mom died while he was in protective custody. Dad is nowhere to be seen. The family he's with is great, but he keeps acting out, exactly the kind of child your sister said could be helped by horses. I sure do hope that proves to be true."

He leaned forward a bit. "I wish you'd talk to me."

"I am talking."

"You know what about."

She did, and she had a hard time figuring out if she was angry or touched that he would push the issue. He wasn't being nosy; he just wanted to help.

"Like I said, it's in the past, Maverick. I don't like to dwell on it. I prefer to look toward the future."

He held her gaze for a moment before nodding, then peering down at his hands. "I guess I should get going."

She stood up again, her gaze catching on the roses. "Thank you for the flowers."

"You're welcome."

"They're my first."

A brow lifted. "Your first?"

"Bouquet. Nobody has ever brought me flowers before."

"Not ever?"

Why did her cheeks heat with embarrassment? What had made her admit to such a thing? "Not ever," she echoed.

Something flashed through his eyes. Sadness. For her, she realized. It made her tip her chin up. She didn't need his pity. She'd done okay for herself, despite her past.

"Enjoy them," he said.

"I'll see you later this week when I bring William by."

"Sounds good."

She watched him walk out, collapsing back in her chair, her gaze catching on the flowers again, and for some reason, she wanted to cry.

Chapter 13

He told himself to leave her alone. His aunt was working with her on Fostering Hope, which was what they were now calling the event. His sister had agreed to work with William, the little boy Charlotte was bringing out to the ranch. He hadn't had any problems with Olivia. No need to interact with her. And yet...

The next weekend when she brought William by the ranch he found himself holding Olivia's hand as they walked toward the barn together, Sadie following in their wake, drawn to see Charlotte for reasons he couldn't understand.

"You ready?" he asked Olivia, guiding her down the step of his home.

He'd missed the little girl during his workdays. He'd hired a local mom to watch her. It meant having to drop her off in the morning, but that was okay. He didn't want to burden his aunt with the task, so they'd set up a schedule. Monday and Tuesday Olivia stayed with Crystal, the rest of the week with Mrs. Rulofson.

"But today we can spend all day together," he told Olivia, who looked up at him curiously. "Which is why we're walking to the barn."

He had the whole weekend off, which was great, especially after a busy week treating cattle with Dr. Mariah Stewart, the local veterinarian, then shifting herds to different pastures, moving some off to new homes. Irrigating had taken the better part of three days. Never a dull moment on Gillian Ranch.

"I'm telling you, Olivia, don't grow up to be a rancher. It's a lot of work."

Big gray eyes peered up at him. She pointed ahead and toward the pasture to her left. "Horz."

"Yes," he said. "We're going to go see the horses. But horses come with cowboys and you need to stay away from those, too. Well, rodeo cowboys. But not Uncle Shane and Uncle Carson. They're good guys. But some of those rough stock riders. Whew. Watch out."

He could tell she was trying to understand his words. The longer she'd been in his care the more words she used. Last week she'd added a new one to her vocabulary. *Horse.* It was clear she loved her four-legged friends. He'd bought her a stuffed Clydesdale last week and she'd gone crazy over it. It'd been a battle earlier to make her leave it in the house.

Sadie ran up ahead of them when they reached the barn, disappearing inside. He could see Charlotte's little compact car parked out in front of the Spanish-style building, another vehicle parked next to her, probably the foster parents. He would bet Jayden had walked down from the house.

"There's my darling little girl." Crystal was standing with a group of people, but she broke away and held out her arms. "Come here, you little beauty, you."

Olivia needed no second urging. She all but ran into Crystal's arms.

The group of people turned out to be who he'd guessed. All turned to watch them approach.

"You made it," Maverick said to his sister, thinking her baby bump seemed to get bigger every week. He gave her a hug, watching as Crystal scooped Olivia up.

"Horz," Olivia said, turning in his aunt's arms.

"Maverick," Charlotte said. "This is Jane and Hal and that's William."

"Hi there," he said to the group, shaking hands with William's parents while Olivia continued to convey her impatience with his aunt and her unwillingness to bring her to see her favorite animal. The couple's youth took him by surprise. Not much older than him. And the boy wasn't much younger than his niece Bella. Maybe eight or nine. "Nice to meet you."

The dark-haired mom smiled, jumping when one of the horses snorted in its stall. He tried not to laugh, bending to shake William's hand. "How are you, young man?"

The kid frowned. "This place smells."

He smiled. He supposed to outsiders it did. "You ought to catch a whiff of the cow pastures I've been working in all week."

"No, thanks."

"I was thinking I'd teach Will how to saddle a horse," Jayden said.

"Really?" Will said, perking up.

She turned to his parents. "You don't have to wait around if you don't want to."

"Oh, no, that's okay," said Jane. "I'm a little weird about leaving Will in strange places."

"Totally fine," Jayden said.

"As long as we're not in the way," Hal added, glancing at one of the horses in its stall.

"You won't be," Jayden said with a smile. "There's a patio table and some chairs off the back of the barn. Go take a seat. You can watch from there if you want."

"Perfect," said Hal.

"And I'm going to take this silly girl around to pet some horses," Crystal said, smiling at Olivia. "Would you like that? I'm sure you would. Maverick, Flynn said you were feeding the mares and foals for him tonight. Why don't you take Charlotte and go do that now? Those mares and their babies are so cute."

"Oh, I don't know," Charlotte said before he could get a word in. "I should probably stay here with Will, don't you think?"

"Nah." Jayden glanced over at him and he could see the amusement in her eyes. He would need to have a talk with his aunt and sister when the day was over. They were clearly trying to push him and Charlotte together, though goodness knew why. "Will's parents are here."

"Go with Maverick," his aunt said to Charlotte. "It's really a sight to see all those horses together. And when you come back, have Maverick bring you up to the house. We can go over the plans for Fostering Hope and, oh, I just can't wait to tell you all the latest news. It's going to be great."

He could tell Charlotte didn't want to go with him, but

she also didn't want to be rude. Her mouth hung open a bit before he saw her throat work in a noticeable swallow.

"If you don't want to go, you can stay here." He offered her an out.

"Oh, no." She glanced at Crystal, and he could tell she didn't want to be perceived as rude by declining his aunt's suggestion. "That's okay."

But as he walked her toward the ATV parked off the back—Greenie, they called it—whistling for Sadie along the way, he wondered why his spirits had suddenly lifted. Today she wore jeans and a beige shirt that brought out the color of her brown eyes. She wore her hair back in a ponytail, and the style emphasized the sharpness of her cheekbones. He realized in that moment that she worked to downplay her looks. Loose clothes, tied-back hair, no makeup. One of those women who was so naturally pretty at first you didn't notice it, until you looked deeper, like a painting that took on a whole new perspective when viewed from far away.

Maverick pointed her toward an ATV that resembled a miniature truck with its tiny cabin and wheelbarrow-sized bed. "Go ahead and take a seat. I need to load a bale of hay in the back."

She nodded soundlessly, and when he took his seat a few minutes later she still didn't look happy. Sadie had already jumped in the back, her tongue lolling off to the side, a canine grin on her face.

"Look, if you'd rather stay behind, that's okay. My sister and aunt can be a little heavy-handed and it's pretty clear they want the two of us to spend some time alone together, but I know that's not what you want, and I understand your reasons why, so you won't hurt my feelings if you want to stay here."

Their gazes connected, and he could tell she waged some kind of inner war.

"No." She shook her head. "I would like to see the baby horses. Your aunt's been telling me about them for a while now."

"Good." He smiled.

They headed away from the barn, skirting the bottom of the hills, past the cabin his brothers and cousins used to share, and then across a shallow creek that kicked water onto the windshield and made Charlotte duck inside the cab.

"You won't get wet."

She clearly didn't believe him, swinging her knees toward him so that they nearly touched. This time of year, the creek was pretty shallow. Come winter, they'd have to move the mares and foals to a different pasture.

The ATV rocked back and forth as they rolled over some boulders. "My dad and uncle bought it years ago, when land was cheap out here. Threw every penny they had into it, bought more land when the ranch started turning a profit, added the vineyards when I was a kid." They made it to the other side of the creek. "It's their baby."

"And you manage the whole thing."

He pointed the ATV toward a gate set between a rock wall—a relic of the past. Back when the land had been a part of a Spanish land grant, it was what they'd used as fencing. They'd added new sections over the years, like the one that enclosed the mares and foals. They grazed in a pasture that'd been freshly irrigated, moisture making the air dank around them.

"Just the cattle operation. My brother Flynn handles the horses. My older brothers used to help, but they've got their own thing going now. My cousins handle the vineyard."

"They all sound like big jobs."

"It is, but I wouldn't want another job in the whole world. Just look at that."

He parked in front of a gate, the mares lifting their heads, their foals scrambling to hide behind their mothers. In the distance, trees cast inkblot shadows on the ground. Yellow flowers dotted the landscape, thicker in some areas than others, like lakes of yellow.

"It's beautiful," she agreed.

"When I was a kid, I used to come out here all the time. There's a place in the back where that creek we just crossed cuts through our property. The pond I showed you that first day is part of it. My dad built the dam you saw on the far end. It has a spillway so that it doesn't destroy the creek downstream. He stocked it with fish. Best spotted bass in the whole valley."

She kept her eyes on the horses and he wondered what she was thinking. And why he couldn't seem to take his eyes off her. She seemed so lost in thought.

"This whole place really is amazing."

And so very different from the place where she'd grown up. She didn't need to say the words.

"You want to say hello?"

She'd gone still, and something about the look on her face made him study her closely. Sadness. That was what he saw in her eyes. For herself? He didn't think she was the type for self-pity, but something had upset her.

"They'll come right up to the gate."

"I'll take your word for it."

"You need to meet them."

"Maverick, I don't know how to tell you this, but I'm sort of afraid of horses." She glanced toward Sadie, who'd jumped down and waded in the creek. "And dogs."

"Yeah, I kind of noticed."

"Really? And here I thought I hid it so well."

He laughed. "Not really. So you should at least get a little closer because it's really all about trust. I promise, they won't hurt you."

She climbed out of the ATV reluctantly, and they walked in silence because he honestly didn't know what to say to her. A part of him wanted to wrap her in a hug. Another part of him wanted to ask her what was wrong. He knew he could do neither.

The mares had started walking toward them, and he debated with himself whether or not to show her Smokey, a bay mare he favored. He could point Charlotte in the direction of one of the other horses and her baby. Instead, he motioned Charlotte over. The mare ate quietly on the other side of the wall, just out of touch, a dark brown foal hiding behind her.

Charlotte stumbled a bit when she caught sight of the scars on the mare's body.

"We got a call a few years back from Animal Control. Some so-called trainer had her in his program. They found her bloodied and sore, tied up in her stall, without food or water. Apparently, he'd been trying to train her all night. Those are spur marks on her barrel and neck. The marks on her face are from a wire chin strap, not the kind we normally use, but a piece of barbed wire rigged to the bridle."

She didn't move and he wondered if he'd done the right thing pointing the mare out. Would it bring back horrible memories? What kind of abuse had she suffered? He didn't know, but he wanted her to open up. To find out why, no matter how hard she tried to hide it, her eyes were always just a little haunted.

"We took her in. Nursed her back to health. She was terrified of humans at first. If you moved the wrong way she'd try and bolt the other, and can you blame her? Took us weeks just to get a halter on her. Such a shame, too. She's bred to the hilt. Probably would have made a heck of a cutting horse, but that idiot trainer tried to beat the talent out of her. So we're using her as a broodmare. She gets to have a baby every year and she's happy. Look. She no longer shies away from people."

He lifted his hand to stroke her mane. The mare turned her head and eyed the two humans on the other side of the wall.

"Here." He pulled a treat out of his pocket. The mare slurped down the treat, the bald patches on her face more pronounced with her so close to them. It had never grown back, the tissue too traumatized.

"She's a great mama, too. The first baby we got out of her is winning in the show pen right now. The baby at her side looks even more promising. Isn't he cool with his big white face? Gets that from his daddy, one of my dad's stallions."

The mare had finished her treat and turned toward Charlotte. The other mares had approached, each of them looking toward him. He cut open a bale of hay and started spreading it around, giving more to Smokey than the others. But Charlotte stood still.

"She's beautiful," he heard her say. "Even with the scars."

"Yes. She is." He half turned toward her, dusted the hay off his hands and his shirt. "And so are you."

The air around them went perfectly still. God knew why he'd said the words. They'd just sort of come out. Charlotte wouldn't look at him, but that was okay. He didn't want her to look at him, worried that if she did, he'd say something else, something stupid and maybe out of line.

"We all have scars, Charlotte. Some are on the outside, some inside, but we can't let them affect us for the rest of our lives."

She stared at her toes for a second. "I disagree," she said softly, so softly he had to lean forward to hear her. "I think some scars are so deep you never forget they're there."

He wanted to touch her again, but he knew if he did, she'd bolt. But he wanted to help her. Wanted to help her so badly it was an ache that clawed at his soul.

"The system failed you, Charlotte. I can tell even though I don't know what happened to you, and I don't want to know, don't need to. I do know you're strong. You didn't let whatever it was break you. You help kids, and you help families that want to adopt. You've moved on and I admire that about you."

There were tears in her eyes, and it made his heart ache for her all over again. What had they done to her? This foster family she'd had to endure. Why couldn't she have gotten away? Or maybe she had tried to get away. Maybe that was the sadness he saw in her eyes.

"You're extraordinary. I want you to know that I know that. And I'm sorry for what you went through. So very, very sorry."

She stood there, and it was a moment when he knew he could make a left or right turn. Left and head back to the ATV, leave her standing there to gather her thoughts and regain her composure. Go right and move closer to her, risk something so precious that it took his breath away. Whatever choice he made, he knew that if it was the wrong one, he'd never gain her trust again.

"Charlotte," he said softly, shifting right.

She didn't move.

"Don't cry."

Her eyes glistened when she met his gaze, but the tears didn't fall. She was the type of woman who wouldn't let them fall.

"Sometimes I hate myself for being so scared."

Her words kicked him in the gut because he knew how she felt. When his dad had insisted he ride a steer, he'd been so afraid, and yet he'd wanted so badly to please his old man. To this day his dad had no idea he'd thrown up behind the chutes. He'd somehow gutted it out and ridden that damn steer, but he'd been mad at himself for weeks for being so dang weak.

"You don't ever have to be afraid of me."

She held his gaze for so long that he wondered if he'd upset her. But then she said, "I know," and her words made his insides flip upside down. The sensation was so real it made it hard to breathe for a moment as he stared into her big brown eyes.

He wanted to kiss her.

He lifted a hand, then let it fall back to his side, terrified of making the wrong choice again. She held his gaze and he began to move again, gently cupping the side of her face. That was all, just resting his fingers against her cheek, trying to tell her without words that she could move if she wanted.

She didn't move.

"Can I kiss you?"

She held his gaze for a long moment. Another choice.

"Yes."

He slowly lowered his head, her eyes holding his own, the brown in them having gone dark, pupils dilating as he slowly, ever so gently, brushed his lips against her own.

She didn't move. He took that to mean it was okay to keep kissing her, and it lit a fire inside of him knowing that she had trusted him thus far, that she wanted him to kiss her. He wanted it to be perfect, this kiss. He wanted to make her feel all the same crazy, adrenaline-surging, knee-weakening things he felt.

He touched her lips with his tongue. He felt her jolt, waited for her to move away, and when she didn't, he increased the pressure, urging her, no, begging her without words to let go.

She opened her mouth to him.

It was like galloping through the shallow part of an ocean, her touch as exhilarating as the sting of the wind on his cheeks and the pinpricks of moisture in his eyes and the shock of cold water on his legs. He lapped up the taste of her, shaking with his need to deepen the kiss even more, afraid to move lest he startle her.

She pulled away.

He let her go, but the sudden loss of contact and the look on her face brought him back to earth as if he'd fallen into the ocean. She didn't have the look of a woman who'd been well kissed. What he saw on her face was more like surprise and maybe even relief.

"Take me back."

"Charlotte."

She turned and headed for the ATV. He stood there for a moment wondering what had just happened. Why did she look at him so strangely?

You shouldn't have kissed her, you damn fool.

He slipped behind the wheel to take her back to the barn.

Chapter 14

Her lips tingled. She resisted the urge to touch them as she forced herself to slip into the passenger seat of the ATV. He didn't chase her. Didn't try to talk her out of leaving. Just followed her back, and she wondered what he was thinking.

That you're crazy. That you're messed up in the head. That there must be something wrong with you because most women would kiss a man like Maverick right back. That and do other things.

"You better never tell me the name of the bastard that assaulted you because I think I could beat him black-and-blue."

The words jolted her in a way that had her turning toward him. He was angry. Not at her. At Rodney. A vein throbbed on the side of his head, and his jaw flexed over and over again.

"I don't know what the hell kind of foster family you had that they let someone hurt you, but I hope they're rotting in hell somewhere, too."

She had to look away, his outrage on her behalf making her heart expand in a way so foreign she couldn't quite place the emotions he'd evoked.

"Thank you." She didn't know what else to say, but it seemed so inadequate.

When they arrived back at the stable, she slipped out of the ATV, wanting to say something more, uncertain what words to use. In the end she kept quiet because what *could* she say? His kiss might have made her feel things that she'd never felt before, but that didn't change the fact that her past made her a poor choice for a girlfriend, maybe even a friend.

He whistled for Sadie to get out of the ATV as Charlotte walked ahead. She hated how awkward things had gotten between them. Maybe he'd leave. But, no, she heard him follow her into the barn.

They'd passed Will's parents sitting at a patio table off the back of the barn. They hadn't been gone all that long, Jayden leaning against a rail by the arena, a blousy white shirt resting against her pregnant belly. Will worked with a red-colored horse, making the animal do circles around him while holding on to a long rope. He held a whip that looked more like a fishing pole in his left hand.

"You're teaching him to lunge," Maverick said.

Jayden had retreated to the rail. "Better to be safe than sorry."

Grateful for something else to focus on, Charlotte said, "What do you mean by that?"

"Nothing, really," Jayden said. "Lunging is a way to let a horse stretch its legs before riding it. Sometimes they'll buck and do things that make you glad you weren't on them."

"Has that horse bucked before?"

"Not in a long, long time. And considering it'd take a horde of ogres to get that horse to do more than trot, I'm pretty sure he's safe. But I told him to let go of the rope if anything happens."

The horse's hooves sent up puffs of dust with every step. Will's grin was so big, it warmed Charlotte's heart. This was what she was good at. Helping kids. Not relationships.

"It's good for him to do stuff on his own," Jayden added, her pretty blue eyes sparking with amusement. "It gives him a sense of responsibility. Plus, it will help forge a bond between Will and the horse." Jayden tipped her head sideways, her black hair falling off to one side. "I get the feeling he's had a rough go of it at some point in his life."

The words touched a nerve still exposed from kissing Maverick, though Charlotte tried to hide it. She forced herself to take a deep breath.

"He was taken away from his biological parents, but more than that I really can't say."

"I understand."

"But his foster parents are the best," Charlotte said. "I wish we had more like them."

"You will soon," Maverick said firmly. "If my aunt has anything to do with it, she'll make sure you have a whole list of people by the time she's done with your event."

"That's the truth," Jayden said. "And a horse therapy program would be great for Will. The animals have a sixth sense for humans who've suffered emotional or physical trauma. I've seen them react to our wounded veterans out at Dark Horse Ranch in ways that would blow your mind. You should bring him out here again."

"You'd have to talk to Will's parents."

"I'll do that," she said with a smile. "Out at Dark Horse Ranch we work with veterans, but I've been thinking of starting a program out here for kids. This could work out perfect."

"Miss Jayden," Will called. "Can I ride now?"

Jayden glanced back at the arena, smiling. "Kid after my own heart." Then she cupped her hands around her mouth and said, "Let me help you walk Little Red back to the barn."

Maverick's sister left them with a wave goodbye, and Charlotte wondered if she could get away with leaving, too. As much as she wanted to stay and watch Will ride, a tension she couldn't ignore hung in the air.

"I'm going to grab Olivia from my aunt," Maverick said. She watched him square his shoulders before looking in her eyes. "I'll see you around."

She recognized the look in his eyes. This wasn't just *Hey, I'll see you later.* This was *I'll keep my distance from you since that's what you want, goodbye.*

"Will you tell her I'll call her later?" she asked.

He held her gaze, and she knew he was waiting for her to say something, anything. To make things easier between them.

Instead, she looked down at the ground, tucked her hands in her pockets. "I forgot I have another meeting to go to."

Liar.

"Yeah, sure," he said.

He didn't say another word, just turned and walked away. And she should be grateful. She really should. And yet, crazily, she wasn't.

* * *

Olivia and Crystal weren't in the barn. His sister said their aunt had taken the little girl up to her house. So he took the ATV and drove like a maniac up to his aunt's, only slowing when he realized he'd left Sadie behind.

Son of a—

Oh, well. The dog wandered the ranch all the time. She'd find her way home. Or maybe stay at the barn. But what a stupid thing to do, and a sign of how out of sorts he was.

He'd kissed her. And he'd wanted to do more. But she didn't want him. Didn't want any man. And he'd known that and yet he'd still kissed her.

Dumb, dumb, dumb.

He heard Olivia inside when he skidded to a stop in front of his aunt's house. She was doing her new thing, squealing with excitement. It'd been the most rewarding thing he'd ever experienced in his life, watching Olivia come out of her shell, and it was the one bright spot to his afternoon.

"There he is," Crystal said. His aunt met him in the foyer. "She saw you from the window."

"Hey, pumpkin," he said, walking toward her.

"Daddy!"

Maverick froze. So did his aunt.

She barreled toward him, throwing herself at him and wrapping her arms around his legs. He didn't remember closing his eyes, but it was a good thing he did because they held back tears, and for some reason, he didn't want his aunt to see him cry.

"Hi, sweetheart." He squatted down, pulled her close, burying his nose in her hair. "Did you miss me?"

He stood with her in his arms. Gosh, he'd only been

gone a short time, but she acted like it'd been forever.
When he looked at his aunt, he saw that he needn't have
worried about shielding his tears. She was crying, too.

"I swear I didn't teach her that word," she said.

He hadn't, either, but it was okay. Maverick knew in
that instant that there was no way in hell he'd ever give
Olivia up. She was his. He was hers. He didn't know how
it had happened in such a short amount of time, but it had.

"You do realize, don't you," his aunt said, "that there's
no way in hell she's going back into the foster care system."

"I know," Maverick said. "I have a court appearance
this week. I'll tell the judge then. Charlotte said we could
make it official pretty quickly."

His aunt smiled, wiping at her eyes. "You're going to
do it, aren't you? You're going to adopt her."

He nodded. "It won't be easy, Auntie, but I know we'll
make it work."

"You better tell your dad."

"I will."

"Don't let him change your mind."

"I won't."

His aunt tipped her head sideways, and she looked
so much like his sister in that moment that it was weird
given there was no biological connection to them. "It'd
make things easier if you found yourself a wife."

An image of Charlotte popped into his head, but that
would never happen. And if he was smart, he'd stay away
from her. He'd always wanted to marry a woman whose
first priority would be *their* kids…not someone else's.

"That pretty social worker would be perfect."

"Yeah. Don't think I didn't notice your obvious at-
tempt to throw the two of us together."

"What can I say? I like her."

Yeah, but she doesn't like me. At least not enough to trust me.

"I'll be back up tomorrow," he said, hoping to change the subject. "In the morning, if that's okay."

His aunt was no fool. "Maverick, what's wrong?"

Olivia rested her cheek on his chest. No better feeling in the world, he thought, wishing he could sit down on his aunt's couch and just hold his little girl.

"Did something happen between you and Charlotte?"

Her direct hit had him turning away. "I'm going to head back down. I left Sadie down there. I should probably go find her."

"Fineus Gillian, don't you dare leave."

He winced at the use of his given name. Didn't matter how old he got, he would never be able to resist a direct order given with that tone of voice. He reluctantly turned to face her.

"Sit down."

He didn't want to. There was nothing to talk about. He'd kissed her. She'd made it clear she wanted nothing more to do with him, and he didn't blame her. After what she'd been through it was a wonder she'd been alone with him at all.

Still, he sat.

She took a seat opposite him on a couch. Olivia grew heavier in his arms and he realized she'd gone to sleep.

"You seem different around her," Crystal said. "I've been wondering for a couple of weeks now if you might like her, but then I'd second-guess myself because she's not really your type."

"I have a type?"

She smiled a little, pulled her gray hair to one side,

and sunlight tinged with pink highlighted a face nearly unlined by age.

"You like them pretty and educated. The jeans-and-wrangler type. Smart, but not too smart. Working, but not career driven."

He wanted to deny it, even opened his mouth to do exactly that, but his aunt was about the smartest woman he'd ever met, and as he thought about it, he supposed that was exactly the type of woman he usually brought home.

"But the other night, when Charlotte came over for dinner, you were looking at her in a way I'd never seen before. It got me wondering if maybe I was wrong. And now you're all out of sorts and the common denominator is Charlotte."

"I kissed her," he said. His aunt's brows lifted and he quickly added, "But she told me to stop."

"Good for her."

"She's...different."

"How so?"

He debated with himself on how much to tell her. But his aunt Crystal was a good listener, and his mind was so scrambled by it all that he found himself shifting Olivia so she could lie down on the couch. Maverick took the time to prop her head on a decorative pillow, the little girl so out cold she rolled to her side and snuggled up against the back of the couch.

"This is going to mess up her sleep schedule," he observed.

"Talk to me about Charlotte."

What to tell her? All of it? Some of it.

He rested his elbows on his knees. "She was a foster child, too."

"I figured as much."

"It left…" He searched for the right word. "Scars, the kind that stay with a person forever. I thought maybe, I don't know, that I could help her. Or maybe I felt sorry for her. But I kissed her and it was…nice, but she made it clear there was no room in her life for anyone or anything."

"You kissed her because you felt sorry for her?"

"No." He clutched his head in his hands. Damn it. Charlotte had him so completely turned inside out he didn't know what to think. "I just wanted to kiss her."

He didn't want to analyze the reason why. Didn't want to think too deeply. His aunt was right. She wasn't his type. Not at all. So what in the hell did it matter.

Except…it did.

"You know what I think?" she asked softly.

He had a feeling he really didn't want to hear what was coming next. Forced himself to straighten and look his aunt in the eyes.

"I think there's something there. I think you like her in ways you've never experienced before. I think you're attracted to her despite her being so different, and the fact that she's not who you pictured yourself dating scares the crap out of you."

He couldn't move, couldn't breathe because, well, she was right.

"And I recognize the signs because I felt the exact same way when I met your uncle Bob."

That took him by surprise. His aunt and uncle were the poster children for the perfect marriage. They were the gold standard for what he wanted for himself.

"When I first met your uncle, I didn't want a thing to do with him." Amusement brightened her eyes, a wry smile alighting upon her face. "Timed event riders. Who needs them? Even though I grew up in a rodeo family, I was determined not to marry into one. I didn't want the lifestyle, so when your uncle asked me out, I told him no. And then I told him no again. Every time I saw him, he'd beg me to go have dinner with him or coffee or something. I finally gave in just to shut him up. And then a funny thing happened as we were sitting there sharing a meal—he impressed me with his smarts. He charmed me with his sweet smile. He wowed me when he talked about his plans for the future, including this." She splayed her hands. "I didn't have a doubt in the world that he'd conquer the NFR. That he'd buy his dream ranch with his brother. That he'd make that ranch into a successful business. But he wasn't what I'd envisioned for myself and, man, did I ever fight myself. So, save yourself some heartache." She leaned forward, slapped him on the leg. "If you like this girl, and I think you do, don't let her scare you away."

Don't let her scare you away. Easier said than done.

Chapter 15

Charlotte read and reread the words.

Ex Parte in the Matter of
Fineus Stewart Gillian
For Adoption of Minor Child

Fineus. The name still made her smile, but her grin slowly faded. The paperwork had been filed with the courts this morning, during his first court appearance, a meeting that she'd made a coworker attend in her stead. And as she set the document down, she found herself turning toward the window and fighting back tears.

He wanted to keep her.

So why was she having such a ridiculous reaction? She'd witnessed many foster parents over the years petition for adoption, but for some reason this time it was different and, damn it, why was she fighting the urge to bawl her eyes out?

He wanted Olivia. And she'd wanted that for Olivia's sake. She'd wanted him to be Olivia's daddy because Maverick Stewart Gillian was one hell of a man.

And you turned him away.

With good reason, she told herself. She absolutely refused to encourage a man when she knew she had nothing to give in return.

Except…she *had* given back to him. For a brief, wonderful second, she'd let herself go and it'd been life changing.

She battled with herself over whether or not to call him, to tell him how happy she was about Olivia's adoption. Say hello. Apologize. But she didn't call him. She focused on her work instead because that was her life.

But as the days went by, and the date for the Fostering Hope event drew ever nearer, she found herself wondering how things were going with Olivia. And if he needed her help. And if he ever thought about their kiss. And if maybe he might want to see her again.

"You excited about this weekend?" Susan asked a few weeks later.

Was she excited?

"Of course," Charlotte replied, although that was partly a lie. She hoped like hell the media event would work like Crystal said it would. But she dreaded seeing Maverick. Somehow, she'd managed to avoid him on her visits to the ranch, probably because she'd insisted on doing a lot of the planning via email. And on the rare occasion when she actually had to meet with Crystal, she'd duck in and out as quickly as possible.

"What are you going to wear?"

"Nothing special." That wasn't exactly true. A few days ago, she'd found herself at a department store, perusing pretty shirts and a pair of fancy jeans with sparkles on the pocket and cute Western boots to match.

"Well, I guess I'll see you there."

But just talking about it sent her anxiety into overdrive. She had no idea why. She'd pushed him away and he'd been true to his words, leaving her alone.

The night of the event she felt like a cardiac patient going in for surgery. Her hands shook to the point that it took her nearly a half hour to do her mascara, and the fact that she was even wearing mascara freaked her out even more. She never wore makeup. Yet tonight she took the time to apply blush and lip gloss and even some eye shadow.

She knew the moment she turned into the ranch that the event would be a success. She'd had to follow a line of cars into the place, people parking their vehicles along the side of the main road long before the stables and the arena were in sight. She had to park what felt like a million miles away, the radiance of the lights inside a massive tent like the glow from a lampshade. The sound of music reached her ears before she spotted the strings of clear glass bulbs they'd strung between the stable and the tent inside the arena. Other lights sat around the perimeter, the kind that were stuck in the ground, solar powered. The whole place looked like something out of a fairy tale, and her heart skipped a beat when she spotted the ATV they'd driven to see the mares and foals parked alongside the barn.

"Welcome," said a woman Charlotte didn't immediately recognize near the entrance of the tent. She was so distracted keeping an eye out for Maverick that she only realized belatedly that it was Jayden.

"Oh, hey," Jayden said, eyeing her up and down. "Goodness. I hardly recognized you."

She didn't know whether to be insulted or flattered. "Jayden. Good to see you." She forced a smile.

"Well, what do you think?" she asked.

"It's amazing. Like something out of a Disney movie."

"Wait until you see the inside. My aunt spared no expense."

She wasn't kidding. The big tent looked like the inside of a hotel, so many plants and tables set up that everyone could have taken a seat if that was the plan for the evening, but it wasn't. It was a social gathering. Music, drinks and a few speeches along the way, although she wouldn't be giving any of them. She'd brought in her boss, Mr. Rocha, who'd only been too happy to take on the task.

"Mingle," she told herself quietly. That was all she was supposed to do. Mingle and talk to people and hope like heck that somewhere in this crowd there were a few people who'd want to take on the task of becoming foster parents. Failing that, maybe someone might hear about the event on the news and be inspired to help one of their kids. That was the focus. That was the only focus, she told herself sternly.

She should have known it wouldn't be that easy because there he was, standing by a table laden with hors d'oeuvres and giant glass jars of what looked like lemonade and iced tea. Maverick held Olivia in his arms, the little girl sporting a frilly pink dress and a matching hair bow. She clearly didn't like the black cowboy hat Maverick wore because she kept trying to take it off his head.

"Honey, stop. You're supposed to leave that on Daddy."
Daddy.

For the first time in her life she wished she had a drink,
was half-tempted to grab a flute of champagne off the
trays being carried around by black-coated waiters.

"There you are."

Charlotte jumped at the touch of someone's hand. Crystal. She smiled as she came around the front of her. "I've
been looking everywhere for you."

"I only just got here."

The woman looked like someone half her age tonight
with her hair piled high on her head and wearing a gorgeous Santa Fe–style shirt with a scooped neckline inlaid with giant turquoise stones. She wore a denim skirt
and cowboy boots that nearly reached her knees and
were stitched with cactus and blue flowers of some kind.

"I wanted to introduce you around. There are a few
people I want you to meet. They came specifically to talk
to you about what it takes to become a foster parent."

She feared the surge of adrenaline that shot through
her had less to do with potential new foster parents and
more to do with Maverick being in the same room. She
had to force a smile.

"That's great. Lead the way."

Crystal kept her busy. The crowd grew thicker and
thicker until she had to turn sideways to make her way
through the room. She ran into Mr. Rocha at one point.
Her boss appeared to be speaking to someone from the
press based on the credential hanging around the person's
neck. He gave her a thumbs-up and a huge smile as she
passed. She waved at Rachelle, her coworker, the pretty
brunette smiling in return, and she looked so dressed up

in her frilly white shirt Charlotte wondered for a moment if she'd dressed up for Maverick.

Maverick.

She'd managed to avoid him all night. That was a good thing...or so she told herself.

Someone tapped a glass, and everyone grew quiet. Crystal stood on a raised dais at one end of the tent.

"Ladies and gentlemen," she said with a smile at the crowd. "On behalf of the Gillian family I'd like to welcome you to our first annual Fostering Hope event."

Someone applauded and that grew to more hand clapping until Crystal had to raise her own hands to quiet people one more time.

"I'm so tickled you could come out. As some of you may know, my nephew recently decided to adopt a little girl. He's here tonight with his soon-to-be new daughter and he wanted to say a few words, especially since it's getting close to someone's bedtime."

People laughed. Maverick made his way through the crowd. For some reason Charlotte sank back, hiding partly behind a man.

"Hello, everyone."

She swallowed. Hard.

"I just want to thank all of you for coming out tonight." He glanced at Olivia, who stared at the crowd with wide eyes. "This is Olivia. Say hello, honey." She buried her head in his neck. She heard more than a few "aw"s, including one inside her own head. Clearly, Olivia trusted Maverick implicitly.

So why didn't she?

She shook her head, trying to shake away the thought like an annoying fly.

"She's shy," he said, looking back over the crowd.

"But I wish you guys could have seen her when she first came to us a few weeks ago." He glanced back at the little girl, who wore a tender smile on her face, and Charlotte's throat grew thick at the love shining from his eyes. "She's come such a long way. But the thing is, she almost ended up a ward of the state. I only agreed to take care of her on a temporary basis. But the more time we spent together, the more I wondered how the hell I was going to give her up. And then one day she called me 'Daddy.'"

He stopped and it was clear that he tried to get ahold of himself. His voice dropped an octave. "That was a moment I'll never forget. I knew then there was no way I could ever give her up."

Charlotte had to inhale against the tears that were forming. She would bet she wasn't the only one in the room.

"Of course, I had to convince my dad it was a good idea." Some of the people in the crowd laughed. Maverick turned and Charlotte followed his gaze, spotting Mr. Gillian in the crowd. "Don't worry, Dad. I haven't lost my mind...yet."

His teasing smile faded. "Seriously, though, there's a shortage of foster parents in Via Del Caballo. So my aunt and I decided to do something about that. We're hoping that tonight you'll do more than drink our champagne and eat our food." A few laughs. "We're hoping you'll be touched by Olivia's and my story and the stories of the other foster parents in this room tonight, and that you'll want to sign up to become foster parents, too."

He looked around the room and she could swear he locked eyes on her. She wanted to duck all the way behind the man in front of her, but she didn't. She stood there, looking into his eyes and thinking...

What? What was she thinking?

"Thank you," he said, turning to exit the stage.

The crowd erupted. Charlotte applauded, too, though her mind was spinning at the same time. He was such a good man. Why didn't she trust him?

"Wasn't that great?" Crystal said in her ear.

She turned. She hadn't even known the woman was nearby. "It was."

"The music is starting next. Why don't you and Maverick dance?"

"Oh, no. I couldn't. He has Olivia."

"Sure you can. Someone needs to be the first couple on the floor. Come on. I'll take Olivia. She needs to get to bed, anyway."

"Crystal, no. I should network some more."

"Nonsense." She hooked her arm through her own.

That was how she found herself in front of Maverick. Crystal held out her arms. "Come to me, lovey. Time to go join your cousins and head to bed."

"You taking her to your place?" Maverick asked, but he avoided looking at her, Charlotte noticed.

"Yup. And you're going to dance with Charlotte."

He tensed. She could see it happen even as he handed Olivia off to his aunt.

"I'm not sure that's a good idea. I think I should go up to the house with Olivia. She's never seen this babysitter before."

"Don't be silly." His aunt took the little girl from his arms. "She'll be fine. Dance."

"It's okay if you don't want to," Charlotte said.

"Oh, my goodness, you two. Stop. I need you to dance. The crowd's just standing around."

People were, but it was clear Maverick wasn't anxious

to take her hand, and she wondered if it was because he feared she'd pull away like she had that first time he'd touched her.

She held her hand out.

His gaze shot to her own, questioning. She had no idea where it came from, but she smiled.

His fingers clasped her own.

Chapter 16

Dance, his aunt said.

So he danced. But only because Charlotte held out her hand and he was smart enough to recognize the significance of the gesture. As he led her toward the dance floor, though, he tried to ignore the way his heart beat out of control and how he could feel the soft texture of her hand and the way her fingers flexed when his grip connected with her own—as if she felt the weird jolt of electricity, too.

And, of course, it was a slow dance. He didn't want to pull her close. It was like being in seventh grade all over again and dancing with the popular girl when he had no clue how to hold her. He placed a hand on her waist, trying not to move it, his other hand still holding her hand. He hoped like hell his palms didn't start sweating.

"That was a good speech," she said, her gaze darting to him, but only for a split second. "Fineus."

He stumbled a bit. "I think I like Mav better."

"I don't blame you."

He was bumped from behind and their bodies connected and it was like walking across a lawn and having the sprinkler suddenly turn on. He gasped. She jumped back, too.

"Sorry," he said.

"No, it's okay."

She was looking anywhere but up at him. He wondered if he should just keep quiet, but then she said, "I've been meaning to tell you how happy I am that you're adopting Olivia."

Good, safe topic. "I couldn't imagine my life without her."

They were bumped again. People had crowded onto the dance floor to join them. This time he managed to keep their bodies from touching. But then he felt a small spurt of amusement. Here they were, both of them close to thirty, and they acted like they'd never danced with someone before. Then again, she had a damn good reason for never having danced before. The thought sobered him.

"She loves you," she said. "I can tell."

"Yeah, well. The feeling's mutual."

Her next words were hard to hear, as if she had to work to get them past a lump in her throat. "I can see why Becca chose you for Olivia's dad."

Becca. He thought about her often. Sometimes he could see her face in Olivia's. It always made him sad, but it also made him all the more committed to Olivia's future.

"I wish she'd have come to me for help. You know, tried a little harder to get in touch with me. She could have come out to the ranch. I wouldn't have turned her away. But she didn't, and I feel so incredibly guilty for ignoring her calls. Maybe if I hadn't none of this would have happened."

She tipped her head sideways, whatever it was he saw in her eyes intensifying. "It's not your fault, Maverick. Don't blame yourself. And if you think about it, she did ask for your help in a way. By putting your name on Olivia's birth certificate, she was ensuring her daughter's future. I think deep down inside she knew the direction her life was headed. I think she also knew you and your family were Olivia's best hope."

He had to look away because the words made him so sad and yet touched him so deeply that for a moment he could barely breathe. He had a feeling she was right.

"I wish I'd had someone like you when I was younger."

He met her gaze, surprised by her admission.

"I wish that, too."

She stared up at him, and even though it didn't, it seemed like the music slowed, like they were the only two people in the room. He didn't consciously make the decision to pull her closer, but he did, and she went into his arms willingly and it made him feel...

He closed his eyes. It made him feel like Superman.

"I think..." She looked away from him again. "I think that if I was different, if things were different, I'd be a fool not to grab your hand and whisk you out of here."

She had the look of a woman who'd said something bold and brave, and immediately wished she hadn't.

"I mean, I like you. A lot. I just don't think I could ever..."

He should let the conversation drop. Should smile at

her and change the subject. Instead he said, "I think you could."

She glanced up at him sharply.

"I think if you trusted me you could."

She lifted her chin. "I do trust you."

"Oh?" he asked.

She couldn't hold his gaze and for a moment he wondered if he'd pushed her too far.

"When I was little," she said softly, so softly he had to lean forward to hear her over the music and the din of voices, "all I wanted to do was survive."

She'd done it again, kicked him in the gut.

"You have no idea what I've been through."

"You're right. I don't. And it's wrong of me to think I do. I just wish…" He shook his head. "I just wish things were different."

The music ended, and he realized she looked pretty. Really, super pretty. Fancy red shirt with sparkles along the neckline that emphasized the flush in her cheeks. Hair down. Her eyes big and brown and, yes, sad.

Sad.

It broke his heart and he had to let her go before he did something reckless, like grab her hand and lead her outside.

"Take care of yourself, Charlotte."

She tried to act like nothing was amiss. When her boss came over to personally congratulate her on a successful evening, she smiled and deflected the credit to Crystal. And when Crystal told her later that the local news station would be airing a piece on them, she acted excited. But when a young couple came up to her, people she'd met earlier, and said they now wanted to adopt, she was genuinely thrilled.

Maverick was nowhere to be seen. She told herself it shouldn't bother her, but it did. She didn't mean to ask about him, but when she bumped into Jayden, she found herself mentioning in passing that she hadn't seen him.

"Oh, he left," she said with a smile, waving at someone who passed by. "He said there was no reason to stick around now that he'd given his big speech."

So she'd chased him off. Again.

He's right. You can't even trust someone like Maverick. What is wrong with you?

Someone that she knew with every fiber of her being was a good man. Someone that she trusted with Olivia. Someone that she trusted to kiss her. Once.

Her face began to feel like the walls to a castle crumbling brick by brick. She had to get out of there.

"I think I'm going to leave, too."

She smiled at Jayden, hoping she didn't spot the way her mouth trembled or the way her hands shook. Damn it.

"Oh?" Jayden seemed genuinely disappointed. "Are you okay?"

"I've been feeling kind of yucky all night. Stomach bug, maybe."

"Ugh." Jayden thrust up her hands. "Stay away from me, then. I don't want to get sick while I'm pregnant."

She felt bad for lying, but took a step back to soothe her friend's concerns. "Tell your aunt I said goodbye."

"Sure." Jayden smiled. "I'd hug you, but I don't want your germs."

"No." She gave a little wave.

Running out of your own event and *not even saying*

goodbye to the woman who's done the bulk of the work.
Some nice person you are.

But when she made it outside it was like she'd been underwater. She gasped in big gulps of air, stood there for a moment trying to pull herself together because she realized she liked Maverick. Maybe even a lot. And it scared the crap out of her.

"Are you leaving?"

She about jumped out of her boots. But then she settled back into them. Her heart flipped around in her chest and then swirled around all over again—at least that was what it felt like. She recognized the voice even though all she could make out was the outline of a pair of wide shoulders and a cowboy hat.

"I was just…" She had to suck in another gulp of air. "I was about to leave."

He moved forward, and it was funny because as he closed the distance between them all she wanted to do was run toward him. To hide in his arms. To let him hold her and tell her everything would be all right because deep down inside she knew this man would never do anything to harm her. Not a single thing.

"I thought you'd left already," she said.

She could make out his face now, light from the tent behind her casting his face in shadows but not to the point that she couldn't make out his soft smile or the way his eyes held her own.

"I came back for you."

And her heart just went sort of *oomph*, beating wildly and causing a cascading chain reaction within her. That was all it did and yet it caused a cascading chain reaction within her. Her chest rose and fell. Her legs began to quiver. Electricity seemed to dance through the air.

This was desire, she realized.

"Where's Olivia?" she asked.

"Still up at my aunt's." He was standing right in front of her now, and she saw his hand lift, only to fall back to his side again. "I didn't want to wake her up. Or maybe, I don't know, I knew I'd be back for you. All this time I told myself to leave you alone, and so I did. But the whole time I've been back at home I've been sitting on my porch thinking of you and I have no idea why, because we've barely even kissed and we've never even been out on a date and yet I can't seem to stop thinking—"

"Maverick."

He stopped. She took the final tiny step so that they were nearly touching, and as she stared up at him, she knew she was about to do something she'd never done before. She told herself to be brave. That he was right. It was way past time to put the past behind her.

"Stop talking and kiss me," she said.

He didn't need to be told twice. When his lips met her own, they were gentle, just as they had been before, but she could tell he fought for control. His hands moved up her back, slowly, lightly pulling her toward him.

He tried not to scare her and she appreciated that and wanted to thank him for that because he seemed to understand just what she needed. His kindness prompted her to open her mouth to him, trying to tell him without words that he didn't need to worry, that she finally believed.

His tongue touched her own and it did things to her that made her insides curl and twist and made her gasp. She wanted—no, she needed—more of this.

He reared back, gasped in air and stopped kissing her so that he could say, "I want to take you back to my place, Charlotte. I want to show you what it's like to be loved by a man."

Loved? Did he love her? She didn't think so. It was just a figure of speech, she told herself, but that was okay.

"Take me home, Maverick. Make love to me."

He didn't move. And even in the darkness she spotted the way his eyes widened. Then his shoulders relaxed and the hands at her back dropped. One of them took her own. They turned in unison and headed toward his home.

Chapter 17

They picked their way through the darkness, although the moon shone so brightly it brushed the landscape with shades of gray. He thought maybe she might change her mind as they walked along the road, but she held on to him like someone afraid of drowning.

Still, he felt the need to ask, "Are you sure about this?" when his house came in sight. Sadie had started barking, but she must have recognized his voice, because the dog quieted before running up to them.

"I've never been more certain about anything in my life."

Hard to name the emotions that flowed through him as they climbed the steps to his home. Anticipation, certainly, but also an anxiousness born of a desire to please her.

The brightness inside his home made him blink. Sadie danced around their feet until he told her to stay. He still held Charlotte's hand as he guided her to his bedroom at the back of the house, which wasn't completely dark thanks to wall sconces on the wraparound porch. He loved his room with its hardwood floors and high ceilings and wondered what she would think of it. She had eyes only for him, though, and just like when they were dancing, a sudden awkwardness overcame him. What was it with her, he wondered, that everything felt like the first time?

"I don't want to scare you," he said, turning to face her, uncertain what to do.

"Just kiss me," she said, her brown eyes so big, the pupils so dilated from being outside that her eyes looked almost black

That he could do...*did* do, his mouth capturing her own, and this time she opened for him almost instantly. *Progress*, he thought, but then stopped thinking about anything other than the way she felt in his arms. She didn't kiss him like other women had in his past. Her touch was shy and tentative and yet all the more endearing because of it.

He pulled his lips away, rained kisses along her jaw and then her neck. And this, too, rocked him back on his heels. She was sweeter than the candy bears he used to love as a child. Nothing had ever tasted sweeter.

"Maverick," she muttered, tipping her head back.

Goose bumps had sprouted on her skin. He could feel them beneath his lips. Her response gave him courage to nibble at her flesh, sucking for a moment before moving on, drawing closer to her ear. When he pulled the soft lobe into his mouth he felt her move, and for a second he panicked, but it was just to reach up and clasp him around the neck, drawing him closer.

He didn't remember moving her toward the bed, but when they were there, he paused again.

"All you have to do is tell me to stop," he told her softly.

Her cheeks were flushed. Even with so little light reaching in from outside he could see that.

"I'll take it as slow or as fast as you want it," he added. "You set the speed."

She nodded and he went to work on her shirt, pulling the red fabric up and over her head. They both kicked off their boots. He started to do the same thing—take off his shirt—but she stopped him, starting at the top, undoing one button at a time. It seemed to take forever, and every time her fingers brushed him Maverick thought he might combust. She could have no clue what she did to him, her innocence evident in her eyes, but he couldn't stop himself from groaning when she pulled the bottom of his shirt out from his jeans, touching a spot that sent heat throughout his entire body.

"You're killing me." But he'd never been more turned on in his life. Touching her. Holding her. It did things to him he'd never experienced before, lit up nerve endings he didn't even know he had.

"Oh." Her hands fell away. "I'm sorry."

"No," he said, shaking his head. She looked so worried that he quickly kissed her. "It's a good kind of killing me."

She didn't move and he worried he'd spooked her, so he closed the distance between them, bringing the bare portions of their bodies together. Her heat nearly caused him to gasp again. Instead, he pulled her up close to him, nuzzling her hair with his chin.

"You amaze me," he said softly. "You're so brave. This can't be easy for you."

She leaned back. "You make it easy for me, Maverick. You make me forget."

Did she have any idea how hard it was for him to hold back? How badly his hands shook? His whole body thrummed in anticipation unlike any he'd ever felt before.

She shifted and he felt a hand again, her fingers pressing him there, right there, and he gasped as if it scalded him, and in a way it did. Her hands were like a lightning rod. One touch and he lit up.

He guided her onto the bed, sinking down next to her and kissing her, this time harder than before, his hands skating up her side, but he was afraid of touching her in the wrong way, afraid of triggering memories. So he made sure to touch her gently, trying to show her without words that he wouldn't hurt her. His fingers skated across her belly, which contracted in response. He knew what he wanted to do then, pulling his mouth away, kissing her along the jaw again before sinking lower, bypassing her breasts for fear of spooking her, keeping his lips soft and gentle as he moved lower and lower.

"Maverick," she said again, squirming.

This was what he wanted, her on the edge of control. He wanted her to forget everything about her past, wanted her to start anew, with him. He wanted to show her what it was like between a man and a woman, what it *should* be like.

He pulled on her zipper, his mouth kissing each inch of exposed skin, pulling slowly down. There might have been one moment when she froze, when she felt the cool air on her flesh, maybe, when she realized this was it. He had almost completely undressed her, and so he stopped, waited. Only when she began to wiggle, her meaning obvious, did he go back to kissing her, first on the thigh, then climbing higher, hovering over her lace panties.

He wanted—oh, how he wanted—to pull the lace panties off her body. Instead, he pressed his lips against the fabric. This had to be perfect for her. Nothing had been more important to him in his life, and he shook with the effort of controlling himself. Never had he felt such a keen sense of longing, but this wasn't for him, he reminded himself. This was for her.

He dipped one side of the lace down, slowly edging them off. He glanced up at her. She stared at him through heavy-lidded eyes. Nothing in her body language told him to stop and so he kept pulling and tugging, slowly easing the fabric off, one inch at a time, his lips following the progress all the way down her legs. She shook. He could see her quivering by the time he'd finished. Goose bumps peppered her skin. He followed a trail of them back up her leg, pausing for a moment at the top of her thighs, gently nuzzling and kissing until she relaxed beneath him.

"I want to kiss you there."

"I know," she gasped.

He pressed his mouth against the center of her.

She cried out.

He stopped, terrified he'd done something wrong, but then she said, "No, don't stop," the words a plea, her body opening for him.

He kissed her again. She cried out once more, but he recognized the sound for what it was. A moan of satisfaction. So he didn't stop. He kept going. He'd never wanted anything so badly in his life as to please Charlotte in a way that would show her without words that she could enjoy herself. His own body quivered with need, but he ignored it, watching for any little sign that she wanted him to stop. That didn't happen. She wiggled beneath him, her back arched, and her hips came up off the bed.

Her cries grew louder and louder, and the sound did something to him. The need to bring her pleasure grew greater than his own need. He wanted her to feel the pulsing spasms that came with release.

"Maverick," she screamed.

Her back arched. Her hands fumbled for something, although what he didn't know. He just kept kissing her until she gently floated back to earth.

She shifted, reaching for him, pulling him up. He cradled her, holding her, her heart pounding so fiercely he could feel it against his chest.

"So that's what it's supposed to feel like."

Her words made him still.

"I had no idea."

He closed his eyes, pulled her closer, a sadness overcoming him when he realized just exactly the type of abuse she'd suffered through. How dare someone hurt her like that? He hadn't been kidding when he'd told her he wanted to beat up the bastard who had done this to her. She was too special, too precious a gift to the world to have had such a terrible beginning.

"Thank you," she said softly.

It didn't matter that his own thirst had yet to be slaked. There would be time for that later. Or not. It didn't matter. Right now he wanted to hold her, to quiet the anger beating in his heart, to show her without words that he would never hurt her.

Holding her had another effect on him, though. It soothed his heart. Made his eyes grow heavy to the point that even though he would have thought it impossible, he somehow managed to fall asleep. And even then, with barely a conscious thought, he pulled her close to his heart.

She awoke with a start.

Charlotte opened her eyes, adrenaline sending a jolt to her heart.

Where was she?

She turned her head. Maverick lay next to her and the noise was a scratch at the bedroom door. Sadie, she realized. She must need something.

Her clothes lay in a heap along the side of the bed. Light from outside illuminated the interior of the room and she spotted how ruffled his hair was, though she couldn't remember him taking off his hat last night. He slept so soundly and he looked so handsome lying there sleeping, his face softened by sleep, a darkness sprouting along his jawline. He needed to shave.

And she needed to breathe.

She pulled her clothes on, and Sadie greeted her at the door with a wag of her tail and a canine grin. She headed for the front door, hoping it was all right to let Sadie out. When the dog slipped outside, she did, too, taking a seat on a hanging porch swing he must have just installed. Dawn was just painting the sky with pink and blue hues that reminded her of an Easter egg.

Last night had been a turning point in her life. She'd never been brave enough to be intimate with a man. Not until Maverick. She'd always thought that she wouldn't be able to enjoy the act, but, boy, had she been wrong.

Sadie came back to the porch and sat down next to her.

"What am I going to do?" she asked the dog. For the first time, she reached her hand out to pet the dog, surprised when Sadie tipped her head into Charlotte's hand as if silently saying, *Pet me.*

"I never thought it could be like this."

Sadie shuffled even closer, resting her head on her lap, peering up at her with eyes that seemed to hold all the souls in the world. She tipped her head a bit more, trying to lick Charlotte's hand, and it made Charlotte duck close to her.

"I always just sort of assumed I'd be alone my whole life."

A dog paw joined the head on her knee and she would swear Sadie understood what was in her heart. She scratched her head, the dog's eyes closing in contentment, which gave Charlotte courage to rub her even harder.

"This changes everything," she told her.

How long she sat there, contemplating what had happened and where this whole thing might take them, she couldn't say. She sat there rubbing Sadie and thinking she'd been missing the boat when it came to dogs.

"I think I should take you home with me."

"You wouldn't say that if you heard her snore."

She jumped, turning to her right. Maverick came around the corner of the porch, two cups of steaming coffee in his hands, and Sadie's tail thumped in greeting. He handed a mug to Charlotte.

"Are you hungry?"

She shook her head. "Thank you."

"Do you want cream or sugar or froufrou-flavored stuff? I have it all."

"No. That's okay."

He sat down next to her, and Sadie shifted her head to his knee.

"Traitor," she told the dog.

"I've been thinking about breeding her. Maybe you'd like one of the puppies?"

"You know, I think I would."

They both sat sipping their coffee. She could get used to this. The thought came in for a landing out of nowhere. She could get used to this, but it would change her life in ways she wasn't certain she wanted. He would expect things from her. He'd made that clear from practically the first moment they'd met. He'd built this house for a family and a life she'd never imagined.

"You doing anything today?" he asked.

She'd been afraid to look at her phone. She had a feeling she'd have a million messages after last night's event. But it was Saturday, and, gosh darn it all, someone else could handle an emergency placement or getting prospective foster parents their paperwork. For once she wanted to untether herself from the outside world.

"What did you have in mind?"

"Stay here," he said, putting down his coffee cup and whistling for Sadie. "I'll be back in about a half hour." He bent, and her whole body jolted when he kissed her cheek. "Don't go anywhere."

Chapter 18

A wagon.

That was what he'd gone to retrieve. Charlotte couldn't believe it. The horse's leather harness jingled and jangled, the wheels kicking up small puffs of dust. There he sat, riding high on a bench seat, Sadie next to him, and what looked like bales of hay on a flatbed behind him.

"Wow."

"I thought you could help me feed." He smiled. "And before you think I'm crazy, this is the latest addition to the ranch. My aunt's idea. We're going to use it for parades and holidays. Been trying to hitch them up whenever I have the time."

A hayride. Well, sort of.

"Is it safe?"

"Sure it is. The guy we bought the team from has been teaching all of us how to drive. We've been using it to feed the cattle from time to time. My dad loves it."

As she stood there looking up at him, she admitted he made her feel like a little kid again. Back when she'd been ten or so, before all the ugliness of Rodney and what he'd done to her, her foster parents had driven through Via Del Caballo during Christmastime. The sight of the little town all dressed up was one she had never forgotten. Nor had she forgotten the carriage rides being given by a local horse person. She'd wanted to ride in one so badly, had begged her foster parents to stop, but they hadn't, and to this day she remembered the feeling of keen disappointment. Funny that she hadn't thought about that in years. And that she'd never really realized that the happy memories were part of the reason why she'd settled in the tiny town.

"Come on up," he said, motioning toward the foot pegs on the side of the carriage.

She would finally get to ride in a carriage and it made her spirits lift in a way she hadn't felt in, well, a long, long time. She couldn't keep the grin off her face.

"There you go," he said, helping her to settle down next to him. "And there it is at last."

"There what is?"

"The smile I've been looking for."

She had no time to react because with a "git" and a cluck he sent the horses forward, and she had to grab the edge of the seat to keep from rocking back.

"I can't believe you guys have a carriage."

"It's actually called a buckboard. This is a pretty good-sized one, which is why it takes two horses in the traces. We bought it a few months ago. Been fun to feed off the back of it from time to time. Aunt Crystal swears one day we might need it. She's a big believer in zombie apocalypses."

"You're kidding."

He smiled. "I am. Sort of. It is kind of ancient technology, and good to have around. Been a great hobby for my dad to learn. Good stress reliever to learn something new."

It was a gorgeous morning out, the sun blocked by the mountains to their east, but still painting the valley with shades of pink and orange. She could smell some kind of herb in the air, the grass around them dry in some patches, little yellow flowers peeking up from between tufts. For some reason, she wanted to hug her knees to herself.

"You mentioned before your dad had heart problems. Is he okay now?"

"Yeah. He's fine. Got lucky. Spends his days meandering around the ranch and riding and showing cutting horses all over the country. So does my brother Flynn. That's why you hardly ever see them. They're gone most of the time. So are my brothers Shane and Carson. As I mentioned before, they both rodeo full-time. And my sister lives off the ranch, as you know, and so do my cousins, so it's really just me and my aunt and uncle." He smiled ruefully. "Like I said the other day, Flynn's in charge of the horse operation, so he's probably here more than anyone else. I manage the cattle operation and I'm Flynn's backup when he's gone. Means I pretty much work from sunup to sundown seven days a week."

"Don't you have help?"

"Sure. I have some and my cousins do, too, on the viticulture side. But we're still really busy. We grow hay, too, you know. So then there's harvesting. Hay in the spring. Grapes in the fall. We all help out with that. But even with all our help it's still a big job."

So this place was his life. "I know how that feels."

He glanced over at her. Behind him the trees had opened up, revealing a large pasture and cattle behind a rock wall. She recognized the place from her first visit. Beyond the pasture was the pond he'd shown her that first day.

"Is your job pretty demanding, too?" he asked. "I kind of had a feeling it was. You called me on a Sunday that first time."

"I pretty much work seven days a week, too."

He stared at her curiously and she felt the need to explain. Or maybe she tried to warn him, and to remind herself of how impossible this whole thing would be.

"Every time my phone rings I wonder if I'm about to meet someone like me, or someone like I used to be, a child who has nowhere to turn and no one who will listen to them. I remember what that feels like so vividly that just talking about it makes my stomach turn, and so I'll always be there, waiting to answer the phone, determined to help whoever needs me."

He pulled back on the reins. She had to clutch the seat again, but he never looked away from her.

"You're amazing, you know that? You've overcome so much. I can't imagine what it must have been like."

The look in his eyes pinned her to her seat, made her breath catch.

"It's why I'm so passionate about what I do."

Was she trying to warn him? She had to look away, felt her eyes grow warm, blinked because she didn't want him to see how close to tears his words had brought her. She took a deep breath, trying to get ahold of her emotions.

"And I hope you know," he said softly, "if you ever need me for anything, I'm here for you."

He wrapped the reins around something and pulled back on a lever, which she realized was a brake of some kind. He leaned forward and kissed her on the cheek again.

"I'll be right back. Need to open the gate."

He left her and she couldn't look away, couldn't stop her heart from beating out of control, couldn't help but think if ever there was a man that she could fall in love with, Maverick Gillian was it.

If only.

He had a hard time focusing. Maverick knew it had something to do with what she'd revealed. He didn't have much time to think about it, though, because a few dozen heifers—babies at their sides—were headed right for him, which meant he'd have to move fast.

"Hang on," he said, jumping back up on the seat. Usually his dad drove in while he opened the gate. He hadn't thought this out carefully, he admitted.

"Get up there," he told the team, clucking them into a trot. He hoped to block off the cattle's escape route because escape they would despite the hay in the bed of the buckboard. Cattle weren't the brightest bulbs on the tree.

He managed to avoid disaster—just barely, though. Charlotte's eyes grew wide when the cattle surrounded the buckboard instead.

"Uh, Maverick, they won't jump in here, will they?"

"Get," he told a mama and her baby. "No, you're fine." He made his way back to his seat, feeling better now that he had the gate closed. "Here's what we're going to do. I'm going to pull forward a bit and I'll show you how to open a bale."

"Wait. *I'm* going to feed the cattle."

He clucked the horses forward. "Yup."

"But what about you?"

"I'll be driving the buckboard. See, we don't just toss all the hay in one spot. We throw it out a bit at a time. That way everyone gets to eat."

She nodded, but she didn't look very reassured and it brought the smile back to his face. She clearly wasn't thrilled, but she was game. He admired that about her. Actually, he admired a lot about her. It'd been all he could do not to wake her up last night and pick up where they'd left off. But he'd held off. He'd known with a certainty that defied explanation that she'd needed his physical presence more than anything else.

"Okay, here we go." He set the brake again, getting up and motioning for her to climb over the single layer of bales he'd put in the back of the carriage. "Use this to break open the bales, one at a time." He flashed a pocket-knife at her. "When they open you'll see they break off into what we call flakes. You'll toss two or three flakes out at a time about every ten feet or so. Like this."

He slit through the blue twine, the hay opening with a pop, cattle already lined up in preparation for a meal. They might not be smart, but they knew the drill.

"See," he said, tossing it out onto the ground, where it was immediately attacked. "Shove the knife into one of the other bales when you're not using it. You never want to carry it in your hand when you're feeding in case we hit a rut and you tumble and fall."

She surveyed the bales of hay, hands on hips, nodded and said, "Got it. No stabbing myself with the knife."

He loved her can-do attitude. "Here we go."

He climbed back into his seat, set the horses off, glancing back for the first minute or so until satisfied she wouldn't fall off or feed too many flakes at one time. She handled everything like a pro, though.

"Question," she said after the first few minutes. "What's the point of having them in this big pasture if you're going to feed them?"

"Good question. This time of year when the spring grass is dying off, we like to supplement with hay. It keeps the native grass around longer, which means we don't have to irrigate as much. We try to conserve water as much as possible on the Gillian Ranch."

"Oh. That makes sense."

He pointed the buckboard toward a small rise. On the other side was the stock pond he'd shown her what seemed like years ago. It was full to the brim, the water running out of a spillway to their left.

"That was easy," she said, taking a seat next to him.

"You did good." He smiled as they crested the hill.

"Oh, wow," she said, having spotted the miniature lake.

"I'm going to pull the horses in so they can drink."

"You're going to *what*?"

"Relax. The horses are used to it. We're not going to float away or anything."

She didn't look convinced, but he noticed she rubbed her arms.

"Itchy?"

"Yeah," she said.

"It's the hay."

"Oh, great."

"Why do you think I had *you* do it?" he teased with a grin.

She pretended to swat at him, but she smiled, and Maverick thought there was no better way to spend a day with someone out here on the ranch. The horses knew where they were going. They'd done it before dozens of times, their legs kicking up water as they splashed into the pond. He turned them left, before pulling them to a stop.

"I've got to admit, Maverick, it's pretty amazing out here."

Yes, it was. "When I was a kid I used to love coming here to swim. We'd make a day of it, my brothers and cousins. Sometimes, in the summer, we'd all race out here. There's a swing in that tree over there. Lots of fun times diving off it, and a few bruises, too, when we landed wrong. It was a blast."

She stared across the water's surface. A fish came up for air, sending ripples toward the shore. "Olivia is a lucky little girl."

"I'll take good care of her, Charlotte."

She held his gaze. "I know you will."

He was leaning in for a kiss before he could stop himself, and she immediately returned it, and it made his whole body quicken. He pulled her closer, and before he knew it, things were moving faster and he pulled her into his lap as the ache to have her returned full force. She seemed less tentative today, more aggressive than passive.

He pulled his lips away. "You're killing me."

She drew back, peering down at him, her legs hanging off the back of the seat. "You never pressured me last night to, ah, well, to finish things for you."

"And I never will," he said, trying to move her off him despite the ache in his groin.

She refused to move, and when she peered around them, he knew what she meant to do. "No. That's okay.

We're out in the open and I know how uncomfortable that might make you."

"Oh, I know." Her hair was loose around her shoulders. She had a bit of hay stuck in it. He reached up and tenderly removed it. "I'm feeling brave this morning for some reason."

"But someone might see us."

"When was the last time someone bothered you way out here?"

He shrugged. "Never. Or at least not in a long time."

"And I doubt it will happen now." He saw her take a deep breath. "I've never felt more at ease than I do here, Maverick. Free. Maybe even a little crazy."

Still, he didn't move, waited for her to be the instigator. And she was, her fingers pulling at the snap of his jeans, then the zipper. He lifted his hips, helping her to pull his jeans down. Never mind the boots. And to his surprise, her fingers grew more frantic the more naked he became. She undid her own pants next, sliding them off her legs, boots and all. She was standing above him, naked from the waist down, and he wondered if she'd change her mind, but she just smiled softly, slipping first one leg and then the other around him.

They touched. Intimately touched. And he froze even though all he wanted was to slide inside of her.

"I don't have a condom with me."

"I'd be disappointed if you did," she said with a husky voice. "Something tells me, though, that you're not very sexually active. And I'm on birth control to regulate things. So I guess the bigger question is, do I need to worry?"

"No," he gasped because, damn it all to hell, he felt ready to explode. "No. It's been…" He tried to think. "A long time for me."

"And this is a first for me."

A first for what? For her to straddle a man?

But then he couldn't think.

She'd slid herself along the length of him and he didn't think he could take it anymore. Last night, coupled with the realization that she trusted him enough to do something so brazen, almost finished him off right then and there. Instead, he leaned back against the seat, gasping when she did it again and again, her lips finding his mouth, her hands cupping the back of his head as she kissed him with the same rhythm as she rode him.

"Make love to me, Maverick," she whispered against his mouth. "Show me what it's supposed to be like."

Good Lord, she had him dying a slow death. Had him moving his hips up and down and kissing her and touching her more deeply than he'd ever touched a woman before. All too quickly they both cried out together, the two of them lost in a pleasure so deep all they could do was wrap their arms around each other, holding on for dear life as pleasure took them to a place they never would have thought possible.

Reality returned far too quickly, though. Birds chirped. One of the horses had grown impatient, pawing in the water. A cow mooed in the distance.

Dear God in heaven, what had just happened? That hadn't felt like making love. That had felt different. Deeper than anything he'd ever experienced before, their hearts and minds and souls so in tune with each other it took his breath away.

Was this what love felt like? he wondered. Something told him it was, and the thought scared him to death.

Chapter 19

They cleaned up at home. Maverick made them break-fast. Charlotte resisted the urge to glance at her phone, but it beckoned her. Like a scary movie she just couldn't seem to look away from, she finally gave up and retrieved her cell phone from his bedroom.

Ten missed calls. She winced, checked her text messages. There were five text messages, three from Rachelle, each sounding more and more frantic because she couldn't find anyone to care for three kids pulled from negligent parents late last night. Two were from her boss, Mr. Rocha. One asking if she'd left the party already, another asking her to meet with him later in the week. She pressed the voice mail button, not surprised to hear Rachelle's voice.

"What's the matter?" Maverick asked when she walked into the kitchen, where he was cleaning up.

"I have to go to work."

She expected him to protest, and for a moment she thought he might, but he nodded. "Never a dull moment."

It hit her then just how badly she wanted to stay, to pretend for a little while longer that they weren't two people with completely opposite goals in life—him to settle down on his ranch with a family, her to go out into the world and help as many kids as she could.

"Dinner tonight?" he asked.

Her stomach did this weird kind of spasm followed by a shot of adrenaline. More of what they'd done earlier? She wanted that. It surprised her how much, given everything in her past.

"That would be nice."

He smiled, came forward. She lifted her head to meet him halfway for a kiss.

Yes. She could definitely get used to this.

"Thank God," Rachelle said when Charlotte called her back. "I have been freaking out. Nobody is answering their phone."

"I'm sorry, Rachelle. My battery died. I just turned on my phone."

Liar.

"Are you coming in? Because I am having a hell of a time trying to place these three kids. And, Charlotte, they're in terrible shape. Filthy. I think one of them might have lice. I need help managing all three."

And so it went. They might be a small town, but they were always busy.

It took her most of the day to get the three kids cleaned up and in new clothes. She called everyone on her list to see if they could take all three kids, but most of her foster parents were already full up, and three at one time was a lot to ask. She found herself remembering that young couple she'd met last night and, rolling the dice, decided to give them a call and ask if they'd considered emergency placement. To her surprise, they said yes.

Dinner? That would never happen. It would take hours to get her new foster parents approved and the kids settled. So she sent Maverick a text message asking to reschedule. As she waited for his reply, she wondered if maybe it wasn't a good thing that she would miss dinner with him. This was her life. This crazy, chaotic mess where personal needs took a back seat. So when he replied back that she should come over on Sunday, she told him she'd see how it went. It was a process to get people approved for emergency placement, as he well knew, and so she told him she couldn't make any promises.

She should have known he wouldn't take no for an answer. When she told him she was working on Sunday, he swung by the office, Olivia in tow, a bag of what smelled like fried chicken in his hand.

She could have kissed him.

"Why don't you go over there and play?" he asked Olivia, who had already spotted the tiny play area Charlotte had set up in a corner of her office for just that reason.

"I could kiss you," she told him, taking the bag from him.

"I think I'll take you up on that offer." He bent and kissed her, but on the cheek, and she tried to contain her disappointment.

"I don't think I've eaten all day."

He slowly sank into the chair in front of her desk and she caught a whiff of his musky scent, the man no less handsome today in a denim shirt and matching jeans and a straw cowboy hat. She sat down, too, but this time the barrier of wood and glass did little to protect her from the pull of the attraction. She'd kissed that mouth. She'd touched those wide shoulders. She'd done other things, too, things she wouldn't have believed possible a few weeks ago, but she had, and it'd been life changing for her.

"Nobody should ever be so busy that they don't have time to eat." He took off his hat, the gesture so reminiscent of the first day she'd met him that the memory pricked her heart.

"Welcome to my world," she said, opening the bag and inhaling. Her stomach instantly grumbled. Just as she'd suspected. A box of fried chicken.

"Thank you," she gushed.

Olivia must have found something exciting because she cried out, "Daddy!" and came running over. Well, as much as a one-and-a-half-year-old could run. It was a white plastic unicorn, rainbow mane and all, and she held it up to him.

"Horz." She smiled, waving it at him.

He turned, giving the little girl his attention, and Charlotte's throat grew thick. Good Lord, what was it about this man and this little girl that made her insides feel like a bowl of pudding.

"Yes, it is a horse." He swiped a lock of wispy brown hair away from her face. "Sort of. It's called a unicorn."

She stared up at him in such a way that Charlotte could tell she was trying to understand his words. "Corn," she said.

"Un-i-corn."

"U-corn," she repeated. Then she turned and ran off as quickly as she'd come.

Charlotte could only smile.

"Are you really this busy all the time?"

She nodded. "We get kids at all hours of the day and night. Weekends and weekdays. Sometimes it's just a temporary thing. Other times, like in Olivia's case, it's more permanent. Then there's the follow-up visits, the wellness checks, court appearances, helping a new parent."

Like him.

She didn't need to say the words out loud, but she could see in his eyes that he remembered the dinner they'd once shared. He leaned forward, resting his elbows on his knees.

"But surely you have some free time every now and then," he said.

Not even forty-eight hours and already she could tell her work life bothered him. "Of course I do. It's just subject to change at a moment's notice."

"So when will I get to see you again?"

"This week," she said. "I promise. We had three new kids to place this weekend. I'll take some comp time tomorrow or the next day."

That seemed to smooth things over, and they talked about all the calls she'd gotten over the weekend. They discussed Olivia for a bit, and Maverick got up and left eventually. Charlotte watched him drive off and wondered if she might have found someone at last.

The thought came to her again when, later that week, they made love with an intensity that left tears in her eyes. Afterward, she found herself shaking and crying.

"What's wrong?" he asked.

She couldn't answer at first, her mind so filled with conflicting emotions it was hard to figure out what she was thinking, much less feeling.

"I guess I just never thought…" She buried her face in the crook of his neck and he pulled her up against him tight. "I never thought I would feel this way, that I *could* feel this way."

He slowly released her, leaning up on one elbow to peer down into her face, and there was such kindness there a sob caught in her throat all over again. He lifted a hand, stroking her hair.

"He really did a number on you, didn't he?"

She nodded mutely.

"And you had no one to turn to, no one you could trust, not even the people whose job it was to make sure you were okay."

She wiped at her eyes. "It's why I do what I do." She took a deep breath. "No one would believe me. My foster parents' son was so good at convincing his mom and dad that he was a perfect angel, and then one night, when my foster mom and dad were out, he…he…"

"Shh," he said. "It's okay. You don't have to tell me."

But it was as if the words, once they started to flow, couldn't be stopped. "I tried fighting him off, tried to scream. We were alone. Rodney was almost eighteen, old enough not to need a babysitter and to keep an eye on me, but I knew he had something planned. I begged them not to leave me, but they just brushed me off." She felt another sob catch in her throat. "I gave up arguing and locked myself in my room, and I thought maybe they were right. Maybe I was just imagining the way he touched me and the look in his eyes, but then…"

Even to this day she had a hard time talking about what he'd done to her.

"Afterward he told me to clean up. Called me a slut and a whore and said it was all my fault he couldn't keep his hands off me. And he just left me there, alone. I knew…I knew I wasn't the one to blame, and when my foster parents came home, I told them what had happened. They brushed me off, told me their son would never do such a thing, and when they brought him down for questioning, he denied it all."

She met his gaze, and there was such a look of sadness in his eyes it started the tears flowing again.

"I tried telling my caseworker, but I was so ashamed I couldn't get the words out. In hindsight, I should have gone to a hospital, filed a police report, but I was young and stupid, and I kept thinking sooner or later my foster parents would believe me. I grew depressed. I thought about taking my own life. Nobody noticed how depressed I'd become, or maybe they didn't want to notice, but to this day I don't understand how my caseworker couldn't tell something was going on. I know she was busy and probably overworked like we all are, but she didn't notice. Nobody cared."

"I care."

"I know you do. And I survived, Maverick. I don't know how I did it, but I survived. I put extra locks on my door. I made sure I was never alone with Rodney again. The minute I was eighteen I was out of there, and the thing of it was, I heard a couple years ago that Rodney had been arrested for attempted rape, and I thought, at last…at last my foster parents will know I was telling the truth all those years ago. But they bailed him out of jail, hired an expensive lawyer to defend him. They're just so blind."

"Shh," he said. "Just shh."

She started crying again, hadn't realized the tears were falling until he wiped one away.

"Those people don't deserve to call themselves parents." He kissed the top of her head. "They should be brought up on charges of child abuse."

"I know, right? Unfortunately, the statute of limitations has expired. I keep telling myself that one day they'll pay for their blindness, but I've had to let go of my anger and my need for revenge. I focus on my job and the children I'm helping, and I do everything in my power to make sure they know that I'll always be there for them."

"Of course you will." He kept stroking her head and it felt so good. Being in his arms was a comfort she'd never experienced before. "You're the most remarkable woman I've ever met."

He kissed her head again, and when she finally relaxed enough to fall asleep, it was the first time in her life she'd felt safe and content and...loved.

They said their goodbyes the next morning and she wondered if this would be their new routine. She'd spend the night, and in the morning he'd head out to take care of his ranch duties after dropping Olivia off, and she'd drive into the office to face another busy day. Only this morning she wasn't headed into work. Well, she was, but she was having a breakfast meeting with Mr. Rocha at the local coffee shop to discuss doing another Fostering Hope event, this one in a different city.

"Charlotte," he said, standing when he spotted her walking toward him. "Have a seat," he said after shaking her hand.

She liked her regional director. As a man in a predominately female-dominated industry, he'd always proved to be kind and thoughtful. He'd gotten grayer since he'd become her boss, she noticed, and she wondered if he pulled some of the same hours she did.

"Thanks for meeting with me," he said.

They both ordered, but Charlotte's appetite had faded when she'd spotted the look on Mr. Rocha's face. He seemed more serious than usual. Or maybe it was just the contrast between now and when she'd last seen him at the party. He'd been all smiles then.

"Charlotte, I asked you here this morning to discuss a promotion."

A promotion?

"Really?" she said, unable to hide her surprise. "That's great."

"As you know, we're really pleased with the success of Fostering Hope. That's part of why we're here. One of the pieces that aired was seen by someone at the state office. They were impressed, even more so when they heard about the results and how well you've done here in Via Del Caballo since you've been hired. You brought in what—over a dozen potential foster parents? That's pretty amazing."

She smiled up at the waitress who brought her an orange juice before saying, "Yes, but I really didn't have a whole lot to do with planning the event. That was all Crystal Gillian. She was amazing to work with."

"We know." He smiled, taking a sip of his coffee. "And we've sent Mrs. Gillian a personal note of thanks. The media traction we've received was an added bonus. That young couple you recruited were great on camera. Their interview really tugged at the heartstrings."

"I was just happy to get them on board. I think they're going to make great foster parents."

"And that's what you do so well. Pull people out of thin air. Like Maverick Gillian."

"Me?"

"We'd like to offer you a regional director's position, Charlotte. Your work in Via Del Caballo has been outstanding and it hasn't gone unnoticed."

If he'd told her she'd just won the lottery she couldn't have been more surprised. A promotion.

"It would require relocating, of course, but we discussed that potential when we first hired you and I seem to recall you were okay with that."

"Yes," she said, her voice sounding hoarse even to her own ears. Charlotte cleared her throat. They had discussed her willingness to leave Via Del Caballo. But that was before...

Maverick.

"Well, good," Mr. Rocha said. "The job's in San Jose. Your salary would increase, of course, and you'd be managing the entire Bay Area. It's a huge promotion and we hope you'll consider it."

"When would you need to know?"

He shrugged. "Sooner rather than later, although I'm surprised. I thought you'd leap at the chance."

"I'm flattered, of course, but I'd want to think about it. I'm happy here in Via Del Caballo."

Happy with Maverick.

"No, no. I understand."

They discussed what the transition would look like, including housing and her job duties, but deep inside Charlotte's head spun. Regional director. A bigger city. A chance to help more kids than she'd ever dreamed possible. Her boss was right. A year ago she'd have leaped at the chance, but now...

Maverick sensed her mood when she arrived at his place later that night. He'd cooked for her again, as he always did, his ability to time her arrival with putting dinner on the table something she marveled at. Tonight he'd made her and Olivia some kind of pasta salad, but she wasn't hungry, which he instantly noted.

"Bad day at work?" he asked.

"No, actually. It was good." She took a deep breath, smiled when she caught sight of Olivia stuffing a handful of bowtie pasta in her mouth. "I got offered a promotion. Regional director."

"Wow," he said, taking a bite of food. "That's great."

Was it? It didn't feel great.

She tried to eat, ended up pushing food around her plate.

"What's the matter?"

She gave up trying to eat and set her fork down. "The position is out of the Bay Area."

It took him a second to register the words, but she saw the exact moment the implication of what she'd just said hit him because his eyebrows shot up just before his whole face went slack.

"But you can work remotely, right? Like out of your office?"

Even Olivia had stopped eating, seeming to sense the mood in the room. She stared between the two adults.

"Well, no," she said, and she could hear the breathlessness of her own voice. "This would require me to move."

Chapter 20

She'd blindsided him.

"Move?"

She nodded, and she wouldn't look him in the eyes. That more than anything told him how utterly serious she was.

"When?" he asked.

"Soon." She sat up a little straighter in her chair, and he saw the way her chest expanded when she took a deep breath. "They want an answer right away. Apparently, there's another person in the wings if I decline."

He pushed his plate away. "And are you?"

Her gaze hooked his own. "Am I what?"

"Are you going to take it?"

She went back to looking at her plate of food again. He supposed that was answer enough. He put his hands in his lap because they'd begun to shake. What he wanted to do was shoot up from the table and tell her no. She couldn't leave. He'd only just started to break through to her. Last night, after they'd made love, when she'd finally told him what had happened all those years ago, he'd felt something click inside of him, something that had made him think...

"Don't go."

She glanced up again, and he could see the pain in her eyes. He knew she could tell her decision was killing him inside.

"I have to."

"No. You don't."

"Maverick, I do." Her smile was bittersweet. "Don't you get it? This is what I've been working for my entire life. At a regional level I'll be able to help hundreds of kids. I would be in a position to help children like me, kids who don't have an advocate, kids who are silently crying out for help and who need someone like me, someone that can see."

His fingernails dug into the flesh of his palms. He found himself staring at his hands as if he could make the pain stop by looking down at it, except he realized the pain he felt came from his heart.

"What about Olivia?"

The little girl looked at him when she heard her name. She smiled. "Daddy."

Charlotte smiled, too, but her grin was no longer bittersweet; it was resigned. "She'll be fine."

"Finish your dinner," he told the little girl. From somewhere deep inside he mustered up his own smile, one meant to defuse the tension Olivia seemed to sense in the air. "Go on."

They both watched as Olivia picked up her spork, getting more of the pasta salad on the floor than in her mouth. He should help her eat except he couldn't seem to move.

"Maybe it's better this way," he heard Charlotte say.

"What do you mean?"

"Maybe it's better that I leave now before things get too…"

Serious.

She didn't need to finish the sentence, and he wanted to yell that things were already serious. That she'd touched him with her tearful story of her childhood and her sudden attachment to his dog and her capacity to love children that weren't even her own.

"So that's it?" he asked. "You're telling me it's over? You're not even going to try and make a long-distance relationship work?"

It was impossible to pinpoint all the emotions in her eyes. Sadness. Resignation. Maybe even disappointment. In him? Why? Because he didn't just clap her on the back and say "see ya"?

"Maverick, we both know this would never have worked out."

Did they? That was news to him. He'd thought they were working through her issues. He'd thought… Damn it. He'd thought they might be falling in love.

"You don't want to be involved with a workaholic like me. Right now it's all new and exciting and wonderful, but sooner or later my late nights and crazy weekends would get to you."

"You don't know that. How could you? You've never even been in a relationship before."

She winced and he knew his words had stung, but he couldn't seem to help himself.

"I'm sorry," he said. "I'm upset because I don't agree

with you. I think what we have here is pretty special, and I just can't believe you're willing to walk away."

She leaned forward. "I was always willing to walk away," she said. "My kids are my first priority. They're the relationships I'm in. My job is my married life. I give it my all. There's no room for anything else."

There was, he wanted to say. She was wrong.

"I should probably go."

"No, stay." He shook his head. "Let's talk it out. I don't want you leaving when you're hurt and upset."

She stood. "What else is there to talk about, Maverick? I'm going to take it."

"But I'm falling in love with you."

The look in her eyes grew sad. "No, you're not. You're confusing love with pity."

"You're wrong," he said.

"Then why don't you move up to the Bay Area with me."

His mouth dropped open. "You know I can't do that."

"How is that any different than what you're asking of me?"

"Because it is."

"No." She shook her head. "It's not." She moved forward. "Goodbye, Maverick."

"Charlotte, wait."

Olivia started to cry. He wanted to follow Charlotte out the door, but he couldn't leave Olivia in distress. By the time he got Olivia out of her booster seat and to the front door, Charlotte was already in her car.

She didn't even wave when she drove away.

"Why, you look like your best friend died," his aunt said the next morning. Frankly, he didn't remember driving to her house.

"Aunnie," Olivia cried, holding out her arms.

"Come here, sweetheart," Aunt Crystal said with a wide grin. "Look at you in your pretty pink shirt. So cute."

He couldn't muster a smile. His aunt had clearly noticed. She motioned for him to follow her inside, and even though he was supposed to be dropping Olivia off so he and Flynn could go gather cows, he found himself doing as she asked. Truth be told, he kind of needed to unload on someone.

"Go on and play with your house," Crystal told Olivia, setting the child down. The little girl immediately ambled toward the giant dollhouse shared by all the Gillian kids over the years. It was taller than she was and packed with tiny pieces of furniture, and just looking at it brought back childhood memories. Now all the Gillian grandkids played with it. Crystal headed for the couch nearby, one set beneath a wide picture window.

"Okay, what happened?" she asked, settling down and patting an open spot next to her.

It couldn't be a secret he'd been seeing Charlotte. She had to drive right beneath everyone when she came to his house, something his family was sure to have noticed.

"She dumped me."

She didn't seem surprised by the news. To his absolute shock, she seemed amused.

"Of course she did."

"Ouch, Auntie. That's harsh."

She tipped her eyes toward heaven and shook her head. "Maverick, you're like my own kid. I've seen you with all types of women, but I've never seen you with a woman like Charlotte. What was it? Things moving too fast? Did you scare her?"

He huffed out a breath of dismay. "She was offered a job, one in a different town."

"Well, that's not surprising."

"No?"

"She's good at what she does."

Too good.

"I knew you were developing feelings for her, you know."

Really? He hadn't known how he'd felt until she'd walked out his front door.

"Clearly those feelings weren't reciprocated."

"But I think they were."

"She left."

"Because it's hard for her to trust."

He wasn't sure how much about Charlotte's past Charlotte had told his aunt, but it must have been enough because her gaze held sadness and understanding.

"She's had to overcome a lot, you know. Women like that, well, it takes a lot for them to believe in love."

Love?

He stared at his hands. "I poured my heart out to her, Auntie."

"She'll come around."

He wished he believed that. But his aunt hadn't seen the look in her eyes.

He left for work shortly after, thinking maybe he just needed to give Charlotte time. She wasn't leaving right away. Maybe she'd come around to his way of thinking.

The one bright spot in Maverick's week was a call he received from someone in Charlotte's office that Olivia's adoption would be finalized in court that week. He thought for sure the news might draw Charlotte out, but he didn't see or hear from her, and as the court date approached, he began to wonder if maybe he should try to call her. But just what, exactly, would he say?

The day of the proceedings, though, she was there. He didn't know if it was official business that brought her to court that morning, but as he went through the final adoption process, Olivia in his arms as he answered questions and visited with the judge in private chambers, it was hard not to keep glancing at her. She stood behind the judge, and he realized why she was there when they were almost done and the judge motioned her over. She had to sign off on the whole deal. Once she did the judge smiled at everyone around him, picking up his gavel and proclaiming Olivia his daughter.

"Congratulations, Maverick," said his aunt, tears in her eyes. She bent and kissed the top of Olivia's head.

His uncle clapped him on the back and then he was face-to-face with his dad. Throughout this whole process his dad had been surprisingly quiet. Maverick had begun to wonder if he disapproved, but as he looked into his dad's eyes, he realized he didn't.

"Son," Reese said softly, "I'm proud of you." He glanced down at Olivia. "This little girl has herself a helluva father."

He had to look down at Olivia because for some reason the words touched him in a way he hadn't expected. He supposed he'd always sought his dad's approval. He never would have thought adopting a child would have given it to him.

His dad kissed the top of Olivia's head, too. "Your mom would be proud."

It was his turn to inhale against tears. "Thanks, Dad."

His aunt and uncle and dad followed him out of the judge's private chambers. The courthouse was old and held the scent of musty papers, their footsteps echoing down a brick hallway and off a recently polished floor. They were having an adoption party this weekend, one to celebrate Olivia's "arrival" into the family. Olivia Gillian. It might already have been on her birth certificate, but it was true in every sense of the word now. He glanced back at Charlotte, wondering if she was thinking the same thing. She wouldn't look at him.

"Here, I'll get the door," his aunt said, racing forward and pulling open one of two massive doors.

"Thanks, Aunt—"

He drew up short when he stepped onto the court-house landing. His whole family stood outside. Shane and his wife, Kait, their twins in a baby stroller at their feet. Jayden and her new husband, Colby, with Paisley dressed in her Sunday best. Carson and Ava, their daughter, Bella, and their new son. His three cousins Tyler, Terrence and Dylan. They all yelled, "Surprise," and Olivia jumped a little at their yells. Maverick reassured her with a hug.

"Look who's here," he whispered into her ear. "All your aunts and uncles and cousins."

And he wanted to cry. More than that, he wished Charlotte was there by his side.

"Happy birthday to you," someone started to sing. Pretty soon they'd all picked up the chorus. Olivia wiggled in his arms. When he glanced down at her he realized she wanted to get down, to go see her new family.

"Hi," she said to them, waving.

They kept on singing, but they all smiled and someone said, "Aw."

It wasn't her birthday. Not really. But he supposed this was a rebirth of sorts.

"Congratulations," said a soft female voice, one that sent a spasm of...something through his whole body.

"Thanks," he said, not looking at her and walking down the six or so cement steps. He took them two at a time and was quickly engulfed by his family. When he glanced back at her, she still stood at the top of the courthouse steps, a manila folder clasped to her belly and a look on her face he couldn't quite understand, not at first.

She looked...sad, and it broke his heart in a way he hadn't known it could be broken, especially when he was the one who'd been wrong. Didn't matter. It felt like his heart literally ached for her. Worse, he didn't know how he could fix it for her. He wanted to, wanted to help her understand that they could work it out. She didn't have to leave.

"Here," his aunt said. "I'll take her."

"Congratulations," said his sister, smacking him on the arm once he handed Olivia off. "I always knew you'd have kids, although, I'll be honest, not like this."

"I know, right?" said Carson, holding out his hand. "Congrats, bro. You're doing the right thing."

He glanced back up the steps. She was gone. He turned slightly and spotted her crossing the green lawn in front of the brick building, all alone, shoulders back, head down.

Someone pulled him into a hug—his sister-in-law Ava. More people shook his hand, clapped him on the back, but Maverick just sort of stood there, numb.

He'd fallen in love with her.

Everyone had turned their attention to Olivia, kissing her, stroking her head, welcoming her into their family. Olivia became more of a wiggle worm, and his aunt finally relented and let her down. She wanted to see his brother's twins, he realized, as she toddled over to them, leaning forward, eyes wide.

"Go talk to her," his aunt whispered in his ear. "I'll keep an eye on Olivia."

He didn't know what to say, didn't know what to do. His eyes must have conveyed his uncertainty.

"Say whatever's in your heart," his aunt said.

It wasn't that simple. None of it was simple. His aunt had no idea what he was up against.

"Go."

He went.

Chapter 21

It was all for the best.

She'd done her part. She'd found Olivia a home. Now she'd move on and find other kids homes. In a bigger city. Start a new life. Do what she'd always known she was meant to do.

"Charlotte, wait."

She didn't want to turn around, but he must know she'd heard him.

"Charlotte," he said again, more loudly.

She would bet his whole family had heard him. Sure enough, when she finally turned to face him, more than one curious face turned in their direction.

"Congratulations." It was all she could think of to say, even though it sounded so trite. Then she realized belatedly she'd already said it.

"Were you running away from me?"

Yes. She flicked her chin up. "No. Of course not. Just

in a hurry to get back to the office. I have so much to do before…"

I leave.

She didn't say the words, but she saw by his eyes that she didn't need to.

"You should join our family out on the lawn."

She shook her head. "I don't want to intrude."

"You wouldn't have intruded. I think my aunt looks upon you as a member of the family."

Yeah, right. She didn't have a family. Earlier, she'd been wondering when the last time was someone had sung her happy birthday.

And look who's feeling sorry for herself.

"Your aunt is one of the kindest ladies I've ever met," she said.

"It runs in the family," he said with a smile.

Why was he always so nice to her? Even when she'd said goodbye. Even when she'd known she'd hurt him, he was still smiling gently down at her.

She took a deep breath. "So, I guess this is it. After today I don't expect our paths will ever cross again."

Salt in the wound. Why had she said the words? They'd caused him pain and she didn't want to do that.

He took a step closer. It was just a tiny step, but the pulse at the base of her neck throbbed in response. There was a look in his eyes, a softness that seemed unique to Maverick, and it always had the same effect on her. It both alarmed her and made her want to melt at his feet.

"Why are you trying so hard to push me away?"

His words robbed her of speech. It robbed her of thought for a second, too.

"This whole job thing. It's ridiculous. We can still see each other. I'm not going anywhere, you know." His hand lifted to her cheek. His touch had the ability to freeze and then send her pulse into a rapid beat. "I realize you don't believe that, not deep down inside where it counts, but it's true. I love you."

She thought she might have misheard him. "What?"

"I love you," he said with a tender smile. "But even if you never believe in that love, even if you want to throw that love away, it won't matter. I'll still love you. You'll still be my friend. My family will always be there for you, too. You don't have to do all this alone."

Her vision blurred. She had to look away, so she took a step back and his hand fell back against his side. She stared at the ground. He didn't know her well enough to love her. When would he understand that? She wasn't lovable.

She straightened.

Where had that thought come from?

"You can push me away if you want," he added. "But don't push my family away. They love you, too."

He tipped back his cowboy hat, took a step away, and she wanted—oh, how she wanted—to call him back to her when he turned around and walked away. But she couldn't. She just couldn't seem to do it, no matter how much it broke her heart to let him go. She had a new future to face, one without him. And that was for the best.

Wasn't it?

Chapter 22

It was not, Maverick thought, a good week. He'd hoped… Oh, how he'd hoped that Charlotte would change her mind. But as the day of her departure came and went, he admitted to himself the truth. She really was gone.

He threw himself into his work. They'd been moving cattle all week, some going off to auction, some to other ranches, trying to make room for the spring calves that'd been born. But one thing after another had gone wrong. A tire had blown. He'd gotten lost on the way to one ranch. Then he'd nearly been killed while unloading a feisty heifer.

Distracted.

She hadn't even called to say goodbye. He tried to tell himself to be patient. That maybe once she was gone she'd realize what it was she'd walked away from. He didn't hold out much hope, though.

"Look out!"

Flynn's words had him jumping backward, just in time to catch the back of the trailer door that swung right toward his face thanks to a blast of coastal wind. He jumped out of the way just in time, the door stopped by the side of the trailer, a huge boom startling the cattle they'd just unloaded into a corral.

"Damn, Maverick, what's gotten into you?" Flynn asked.

"Nothin'," Maverick grumbled.

His brother knew what was wrong. His whole darn family had seen Charlotte walk away from him. He wouldn't be surprised if his aunt had shared that Charlotte was leaving town. So far, everyone had held their tongues. Everyone but Jayden and Aunt Crystal, who'd encouraged him to go talk to her before she'd left town. He'd stubbornly refused.

"If you keep this up you're going to get yourself killed."

Maybe that'd be a blessing. But, no, Olivia needed him. She was the most important thing in his life right now.

"It's that woman, isn't it?"

"Don't want to talk about it."

"Why you even interested in her?" Flynn asked. "She's not even your type."

Maverick grabbed the trailer door, then swung it around to close it, but Flynn had the same idea—to close the door—which was why he nearly clocked his brother upside the head.

"Hey."

"Sorry." Maverick latched the thing closed.

"Man, you really are messed up in the head." Flynn

placed his hands on his hips. "And she's not even good-looking. Crazy."

He spun on his brother. "Watch it."

Flynn threw his hands in the air in a gesture of defense. "Just making an observation."

"If you knew her like I do you wouldn't say that."

"You mean something like beauty is in the eye of the beholder." One of Flynn's thick brows lifted, his blue eyes teasing.

He echoed Flynn's stance. "One day, Flynn, you're going to fall in love, and when you do, I'm going to laugh my ass off."

"Yeah, well, don't hold your breath. I've got too many things to do before I settle down."

"Until you meet the right woman, and then it's a game changer."

"Which is why she left you, huh? Too much of a change?"

"Something like that."

They headed back to the truck. Flynn seemed to know when to shut up. They both waved to the rancher who'd just bought ten replacement heifers from Gillian Ranch. But the whole way back, Maverick wondered if he should just give up. The thought made his stomach feel like that time Flynn had sucker punched him.

By the time they arrived at Gillian Ranch, he'd come to a decision. He would call her. He didn't care that she was probably busy in a new town, or that she probably wouldn't even answer and he'd be forced to leave some god-awful voice mail. He would call her, and if she ignored him he'd call her again, and if she ignored those calls he'd go see her. He wasn't sure how he'd find her, but he would.

As it turned out, he didn't need to do any of that. When he drove up to his aunt's house to pick up Olivia later that night, his heart just about came out of his chest when he saw whose car was parked out front. She must have seen his truck drive up the long road because his aunt's front door opened before he'd gotten out, and when he all but stumbled out of his seat he heard his brother say, "I'll see you inside."

Charlotte shot Flynn a half-hearted smile as he passed.

"So, you didn't flee the country yet," Flynn teased. "Interesting."

But his brother didn't give her time to answer. He kept on walking, leaving the two of them alone. And Maverick didn't know what to say, didn't know what to do. It was like confronting a spooky horse. Did he go up to her and touch her? Did she want him to stand there?

Has she moved to the Bay Area already?

"You want to go for a walk?" she asked, pointing with her chin toward the path they'd walked weeks and weeks ago.

"Sure."

His heart beat up his rib cage. He ended up not touching her even though he wanted to with every fiber of his being.

They walked in silence, and when they made it to the giant oak tree and the picnic bench beneath, they both took a seat on the tabletop. Maverick tried to reassure himself by looking out over the valley.

"I don't think I could ever tire of this view," she commented softly.

He looked right at her, leaning toward her a bit. "Me, either."

She swiped a lock of hair behind her ear and he saw that

her hands shook. A breeze caught the scent of her, bringing it to his nose. Lemon cookies. She always smelled so sweet. It drove him nuts.

"Well," she said on a huff of laughter that really wasn't amusement. More like self-deprecation. "As you can see, I'm still in town."

His heart leaped. He hadn't known for sure. Thought maybe she was just back for a visit.

"Packed up my whole apartment, loaded it into a moving pod, turned in my keys to my landlord and just…" She shook her head. "Couldn't do it."

He released a breath he hadn't even known he'd been holding.

She turned her body, facing him more fully. "It took a lot of courage on my part to be intimate with you. Afterward, I congratulated myself on being so brave, but I realized out in front of that courthouse I wasn't brave at all." She shook her head. "I turned into a lily-livered coward when I realized my feelings for you had changed."

"You're not a coward."

Her lips pressed together, tighter and tighter. "Yes, Maverick, I am. What you said to me out on those courthouse steps, when you talked about your family always loving me, when you told me you loved me, I realized I didn't want to believe it. So I went to see a therapist, something I haven't done in years. But I knew I had to do it if I wanted a chance at making this work."

Making this work? Did that mean…?

"I love you, Maverick."

To hell with it. He pulled her into his arms, holding her tight.

She loved him.

It was impossible to describe the way the words made

him feel. Like it was Christmas and his birthday combined and he'd gotten all the presents in the world wrapped up in one package... Charlotte. He bent to kiss her.

"No, wait," she said, drawing back a bit, tears in her eyes. "I have to finish saying this."

He froze for a moment, wondering if he'd gotten it all wrong. If this was really a breakup.

"I love you," she said. "But, according to a therapist, I don't believe I'm worthy of that love. I'm messed up. Of course, you probably knew that, but I do feel I should give you fair warning in the event I freak out and try and leave you again."

He closed his eyes, his eyes growing warm, tears held back by his lids. He leaned his head down until they were forehead to forehead. Then he opened his eyes and stared as deeply as he could into her own gaze.

"You won't leave me, Charlotte, just as I won't ever leave you."

"And I don't know if I want kids."

He could tell that the words had been hard for her to say. "That's also part of what my therapist helped me to see. Part of why I held back was because I knew what a game changer this might be for you, and that scared me even more. I don't know if I want kids. I want to adopt. I want to give kids the kind of home you grew up in. I want them to know love and compassion and the security of two parents who will always be there for them."

"They'll have that and more."

"I know. I'm just afraid."

"I know."

Her face crumpled. He pulled her into his arms again. She started bawling and it was okay, Maverick thought, patting and rubbing her back. It was all okay. They would get through her hang-ups and relationship worries and marital spats because that was what he wanted to do, marry her.

"I love you," she murmured once her tears had slowed. Maverick realized he hadn't even kissed her, but that was okay because their relationship wasn't about the physical— it was about giving her courage, and his arms holding her tight on those days when she feared he'd leave her, and teaching her that love was something you could trust.

Her hands lifted to his face, slowly pulling his head down. Her lips brushed his own, and just like the first time he'd kissed her, what started out slow turned into fast and hard, Maverick trying to show her without words that he loved her, too. He would always love her.

A long while later they drew apart. Maverick clasped her face in his hands again.

"Just promise me one thing," he said.

"What's that?" she asked, a tear falling down her cheek.

"We draw the line at ten kids."

"Ten?" She shook her head and laughed. "I want to adopt, not start an orphanage."

He laughed, too. "I'm thinking maybe four kids."

"Five," she said.

"Including Olivia."

"Not including Olivia," she countered.

"Deal."

Her laughter faded as she looked him in the eyes. "It won't be easy, Maverick. I'm not quitting my job. I love it too much."

"I know, and I'd be disappointed if you did."

She felt her breath catch. "I don't deserve you, Maverick Gillian."

He shook his head. "No, you deserve the moon and the

stars and everything in the heavens for all you've done for kids and all you've gone through. You deserve happiness and love and laughter, and I swear to you, Charlotte, I'm going to give it to you."

She started crying again.

"Do you believe me?" he asked.

She nodded, slowly at first, then faster and faster.

"Good. Because I meant every word."

Epilogue

"Well?" Jayden asked from the other side of the bathroom door.

Charlotte stared at the twin lines on the pregnancy test, clutching the skirts of her wedding dress for moral support. She refused to believe her own eyes. She set the plastic stick down and picked up the box, matching the diagram on the side to the markers on the test.

Dear Lord in heaven.

"I'm pregnant."

The words had barely escaped as a whisper, but Jayden must have heard them. "You are!" she squealed from the other side, and she must have jumped up and down because Charlotte could hear a thump. And that must have been quite a feat in her blue bridesmaid dress and heels. "I *knew* it."

Charlotte turned and mutely opened the door. Jayden

immediately drew her into her arms, something not easy to do given Charlotte wore a wedding dress that would have done a Southern belle proud.

"How did this happen?" Charlotte heard herself say.

"Well…" Jayden drew back. "I'm guessing you and Maverick had sex."

"Jayden!"

Her soon-to-be sister-in-law laughed. "When are you going to tell him? Tonight? When you start your honeymoon? That would be a helluva wedding present."

"This wasn't supposed to happen now. We were supposed to adopt first. Let Olivia get older. Maybe adopt two children before having our own, and now…"

Jayden leaned toward her. "It never happens when you want it to."

"What's wrong?" said Ava, her other future sister-in-law, coming into Maverick's bedroom, where they were all getting dressed for the wedding. They were about to make the trek up the hill and to the clearing above Crystal's house. "You look shocked. Are you okay? Do you need to sit down?"

"She's pregnant," Jayden said, her ice-blue dress flaring at her feet as she spun toward Ava.

"No," Ava gasped. "I thought you guys were waiting."

"She was," Jayden answered for her. "But she's been sick all week, so I made her take a pregnancy test just now."

"On her wedding day?" Ava asked in disbelief. "You made her take a test now? Today, of all days?"

"I couldn't pin her down before now." Jayden splayed her hands. "So I bought one this morning and handed it to her when she went to change."

"You're incorrigible," Ava said with a shake of her head.

"Just wait until you tell my brother," Jayden said. "He's going to faint in shock. Ooh, I get to plan another baby shower, and this one will be even better than the last."

"First we should make sure he marries her," Ava said.

"True," Jayden said. "But I'm so excited CJ will have another cousin to play with soon." She patted her now flat belly. Jayden had given birth two months before to Colby Jr., and these days you couldn't even tell she'd been pregnant.

"Excuse me." Charlotte didn't know whether to laugh or cry. She'd come to love these two women more than she would have thought possible over the past year. "I'm still here."

They both turned to look at her. Ava smiled and said, "Congratulations, Char. You're going to be a great mother."

But she wasn't supposed to be pregnant. They'd had a plan. She'd taken the job of regional director with the caveat that she'd do the job from Via Del Caballo. She hadn't thought they'd agree, but they had, which meant she'd spent the past year busier than she'd ever been. But at least she hadn't had to plan the wedding. They'd had the good sense to hire a wedding planner.

"I think I'm going to be sick," she heard herself say.

"Oh, no, you don't," Jayden said. "You're in your wedding dress. I might be your bridesmaid, but I'm not cleaning barf off that white silk."

"It'll be okay," Ava said, rubbing Charlotte's silk-clad shoulder. "There's a reason why this happened now. Trust me, you're going to be all right."

And as she looked into the eyes of her future sister-in-law, Charlotte knew Ava was right. She couldn't have asked for a better support group than the Gillian family. They *were* her family, the one she'd never had, and it made her want to cry just thinking about it…

"Oh, no, you don't," Jayden said again. "Don't you dare cry. We are not doing your makeup again."

"I think I'm in shock," Charlotte admitted.

"You're pregnant." Ava smiled knowingly. "Your emotions will be up and down for the next nine months."

"She's *what*?"

They all turned toward Crystal, who was resplendent in a floor-length blue gown, Olivia in her arms, the little girl's eyes opening wide when she saw Charlotte in her dress.

"Pretty," Olivia said, pointing. "Like a princess."

The look in Olivia's eyes made Charlotte smile. "Thank you, sweet pea." She came forward, her dress swooshing on the ground, as Olivia reached for the pearls and crystals that covered the bodice. "You look pretty, too."

"She's got a bun in the oven," Jayden whispered to her aunt. "We just found out."

"Today?"

"Today. Thanks to Dr. Estrogen here." Ava nudged Jayden. "Who the heck buys a bride a pregnancy test to take on her wedding day."

"I figured she'd want to know," Jayden said.

"Want down." Olivia started wiggling in Crystal's arms. "Want chocolate."

That was what Olivia called her. Chocolate, and it made Charlotte's smile grow even bigger. Jayden was right. It'd be okay. How could it not be with a man like Maverick and a daughter like Olivia in her life?

"No, no, honey. We came up to get Charlotte, remember? Your soon-to-be new mommy." The shock must have worn off for Crystal, too, because she smiled, although it looked a bit rueful. "She's going to be late for her own wedding if she doesn't climb into that carriage outside soon. Remember? The carriage. You wanted to ride in it."

Olivia's eyes grew wide at the mention of the glossy black vehicle. She'd been begging to ride in the Georgian-era coach ever since Crystal had bought it.

"Let's go," Jayden said. "You can tell Maverick after."

And the thought of seeing Maverick, of walking toward him all the while knowing she was now pregnant, made her nervous all over again. What would he say? Would he be angry? She'd made such a big deal about sticking to the plan and yet somehow she'd blown it. Was it the pills she'd missed taking? She'd been so busy lately. But you were supposed to be able to catch up.

She would never remember climbing into the coach, which had been decorated with Christmas lights. It was an evening wedding. The two of them would say their vows beneath the old oak tree that had remained so special to Charlotte and Maverick, and Olivia clapped and laughed the whole way there. Their wedding planner, Amy, had strung lights all along the path the carriage took. She'd done the same thing to the old oak tree—wrapped lights around the trunk and branches. The effect was dazzling, to say the least.

"So pretty," Olivia said, pointing at the lights.

"I know."

The women of her life—her bridesmaids because, yes, Aunt Crystal was her maid of honor even though she was fond of saying she was hardly a maid—kept shooting her reassuring smiles. But they didn't help. Should she tell him now? Before the marriage? At the altar?

"Here we go," Ava said, helping her stand, smoothing her skirts.

Ava's husband, Carson, handed her down. The men of the family wore black jackets and white button-downs, but they'd insisted on wearing jeans and boots. Charlotte hadn't minded.

"Flowers," said Amy, their wedding planner, the dress she wore barely covering her own bulging belly. "Where are her flowers?"

"Here," Flynn said, bringing over a box.

Her wedding planner took the box from Flynn, the two of them exchanging an odd look that gave Charlotte pause.

"It looks beautiful," Charlotte said, touching Amy on the arm and drawing her attention. "Everything is just as you said it would be."

She watched as her wedding planner took a deep breath. "Thank you."

"You've done an amazing job," Charlotte said. "Really. I don't know what we would have done without you."

"Are we ready?" Crystal interrupted, glancing down at Olivia. "Ready to drop your flowers, Olivia?"

Charlotte gave Amy one last squeeze of gratitude before turning away. Olivia grew excited all over again. She would walk down the aisle with Crystal, and Charlotte got misty eyes watching the two of them set off up a gently lit path that would lead them to the altar that had been set up beneath the brightly lit tree. Shane, Maverick's best man, was next. Jayden walked opposite Shane and then went Ava and Carson. Flynn took the arm of Susan, her coworker, who'd been a rock this past year and had become a close friend.

Then it was just her.

"Ready?" asked Maverick's dad, coming up behind her. She hadn't even noticed him there.

She inhaled sharply. This was it. The moment she'd been waiting for.

"Let's do this."

But he didn't take off immediately. Instead, he held her hand for a moment. "In case I don't have a chance to say it, I'm proud of my son and the woman he's chosen to spend the rest of his life with."

She felt her eyes well with tears, remembered Jayden's stern warning not to cry and took a deep breath. "Thank you, Reese."

They walked toward the giant oak tree. Amy had wrapped so many lights around the massive trunk and branches that it looked like a living lightning bolt. An altar stood at the edge of the tree's massive reach, one covered in more lights that were entwined with grapevines from below. People sat on benches Carson had carved. Bella, Ava's daughter, held Sadie's leash. Colby stood next to her, taking CJ's tiny arm and waving it at her. Charlotte had cried when Carson told her each one of his family members would get to take home a bench in honor of their wedding day. Such a special gesture.

Her groom turned.

And she knew it'd be all right. That things would work out. That she might be pregnant, but it would be okay.

She smiled. He smiled, too. Reese handed her off to her groom. Maverick took her hand. Their pastor stepped forward, an older man who'd married Ava and Carson, too.

"Welcome, everyone," he said with a wide smile. "We're gathered here today to marry Charlotte Bennett to Fineus Gillian."

She giggled at the use of his name, Maverick glancing at her in mock anger, which made her smile. When Jayden started to giggle, too, it made Charlotte laugh, and that set the tone for the rest of the ceremony. Laughter when Olivia insisted on picking up the rose petals she'd already dropped. Teasing when Maverick almost dropped her wedding ring. And most of all…love. Love in the eyes of her groom and in the eyes of her new family and in her heart.

"I now pronounce you Mr. and Mrs. Fineus Gillian."

Which made everyone laugh all over again, and that was how they walked back down the aisle, hand in hand, smiling and waving.

"We did it," Maverick said when they made it back to Crystal and Bob's house for their wedding dinner.

"Yes, we did, but I probably should have told you something before we said our 'I do's.'"

Maverick tipped his head. "What?"

She took a deep breath, and it shocked her how much just thinking the words brought love to her heart. "I'm pregnant."

"Ha ha ha," he said. "Very funny."

She stared up at him with utter seriousness. "No, Maverick, I really am."

He still didn't look like he believed her, but then Crystal arrived with Olivia in tow.

"Did you tell him yet?"

He glanced at his aunt and then back at her, and finally—finally—he started to believe. She could see it in his eyes.

"You're pregnant."

She nodded, and then she felt tears build and she knew she was about to cry. Dang it. She'd held it together through the whole ceremony, but the look in Maverick's eyes…

He pulled her into his arms. "Oh, Charlotte," he whispered softly. "I love you so much."

She released a soft sob. "I love you, too, Fineus."

He kissed her, and the rest of her new family gathered around, and when he drew back, there were claps on the back and congratulations and some teasing because Ava told Charlotte she would have to do her toasting with sparkling apple cider.

"This was not part of the plan," she said as they headed to the backyard, where they'd set up tables for their wedding reception.

"No," Maverick said. "This is so much better."

And it was.

* * * * *

*To give the orphaned triplets they're guardians of the
stability they need, Lulu McCabe and Sam Kirkland
decide to jointly adopt them. But when it's discovered
their marriage wasn't actually annulled, they have
to prove to the courts they're responsible—
by renewing their vows!*

Read on for a sneak preview of Cathy Gillen Thacker's
Their Inherited Triplets,
the next book in the
Texas Legends: The McCabes *miniseries.*

"The two of you are still married," Liz said.

"Still?" Lulu croaked.

Sam asked, "What are you talking about?"

"More to the point, how do you know this?" Lulu
demanded, the news continuing to hit her like a gut punch.

Travis looked down at the papers in front of him.
"Official state records show you eloped in the Double
Knot Wedding Chapel in Memphis, Tennessee, on
Monday, March 14, nearly ten years ago. Alongside
another couple, Peter and Theresa Thompson, in a double
wedding ceremony."

Lulu gulped. "But our union was never legal," she
pointed out, trying to stay calm, while Sam sat beside her
in stoic silence.

Liz countered, "Ah, actually, it is legal. In fact, it's still
valid to this day."

Sam reached over and took her hand in his, much as he had the first time they had been in this room together. "How is that possible?" Lulu asked weakly.

"We never mailed in the certificate of marriage, along with the license, to the state of Tennessee," Sam said.

"And for our union to be recorded and therefore legal, we had to have done that," Lulu reiterated.

"Well, apparently, the owners of the Double Knot Wedding Chapel did, and your marriage was recorded. And is still valid to this day, near as we can tell. Unless you two got a divorce or an annulment somewhere else? Say another country?" Travis prodded.

"Why would we do that? We didn't know we were married," Sam returned.

Don't miss
Their Inherited Triplets *by Cathy Gillen Thacker,*
available August 2019 wherever
Harlequin® Special Edition books and ebooks are sold.

www.Harlequin.com

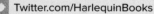

Looking for more satisfying love stories
with community and family at their core?

Check out **Harlequin® Special Edition**
and **Love Inspired®** books!

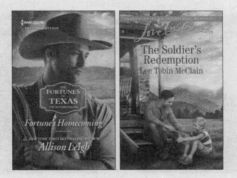

New books available every month!

CONNECT WITH US AT:

Facebook.com/groups/HarlequinConnection

Facebook.com/HarlequinBooks

Twitter.com/HarlequinBooks

Instagram.com/HarlequinBooks

Pinterest.com/HarlequinBooks

ReaderService.com

HARLEQUIN®

ROMANCE WHEN
YOU NEED IT

HFGENRE2018

Looking for inspiration in tales
of hope, faith and heartfelt romance?

Check out **Love Inspired**® and
Love Inspired® **Suspense** books!

New books available every month!

CONNECT WITH US AT:

Facebook.com/groups/HarlequinConnection

 Facebook.com/HarlequinBooks

 Twitter.com/HarlequinBooks

 Instagram.com/HarlequinBooks

Pinterest.com/HarlequinBooks

ReaderService.com

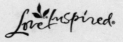

LIGENRE2018R2